"You're sort of a jerk, you know that?"

He clenched his determined jaw. "It doesn't matter as long as I get what I want." He strode purposefully toward her plane.

Hmm. Now Sophia was beginning to understand why that blond babe, usually at his elbow, looked so uptight 90 percent of the time. However, she certainly got the push-pull attraction of Gibb Martin. While part of her wanted to throttle him, another part wanted to kiss him. He was, after all, tall, with handsome good looks and a hot body.

All the more reason not to fly him to Key West.

So why had she agreed?

Blaze®

Dear Reader,

Crash Landing is my final book for Harlequin Blaze in the Stop the Wedding! series. The idea for the series was three road trips as three couples race across the country to stop what they consider to be an ill-conceived wedding. With an added little twist— one road trip by land, one by sea and one by air.

The theme of *Crash Landing* is "money isn't everything" as billionaire venture capitalist Gibb Martin sets off on an ill-fated trip in a Piper Cherokee with spunky bush pilot Sophia Cruz.

Once upon a time I took flying lessons, and I drew on those experiences to create Sophia. My husband is an airline mechanic, so he helped me with some of the technical details about how to crash a plane and then get it flying again. (You should have heard our detailed conversations about ferrules and thimbles.) I've also visited Costa Rica and Key West. I could write a hundred books set in both those fascinating places. Being raised in Texas, I know a little Spanish, but have to admit I spent time on the Babelfish website. Research is fun!

So kick back, relax, get yourself something fruity to drink and let *Crash Landing* whisk you away to a beautiful tropical island paradise....

Feliz lectura,

Lori Wilde

Crash Landing

—

Lori Wilde

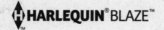

Recycling programs
for this product may
not exist in your area.

ISBN-13: 978-0-373-79749-3

CRASH LANDING

Copyright © 2013 by Laurie Vanzura

Printed in U.S.A.

ABOUT THE AUTHOR

Lori Wilde is a *New York Times* bestselling author and has written more than forty books. She's been nominated for a RITA® Award and four *RT Book Reviews* Reviewers' Choice Awards. Her books have been excerpted in *Cosmopolitan, Redbook* and *Quick & Simple.* Lori teaches writing online through Ed2go. She's also an R.N. trained in forensics and she volunteers at a women's shelter. Visit her website, www.loriwilde.com.

Books by Lori Wilde

HARLEQUIN BLAZE

 *The White Star
**The Martini Dares
 †Perfect Anatomy
††Uniformly Hot!
 ‡Stop the Wedding!

To get the inside scoop on Harlequin Blaze and its talented writers, be sure to check out blazeauthors.com.

To all my readers, past, present and future.
Thank you so very much for reading.
Without you, I'm nothing.

1

THE CRAZY AMERICAN WAS *still* in a business suit?

Sophia Cruz lounged in the hammock outside the exclusive retreat in the Costa Rican volcanic mountain range of Cordillera of Tilarán.

Bosque de Los Dioses, or Forest of the Gods, was accessible only by bush plane and it lay twenty-five miles north of Monteverde, the nearest village and Sophia's hometown. The resort was hush-hush, a place where the rich, famous and high-powered came for a secret hideaway.

Sophia herself was neither rich, famous, high-powered nor looking to escape anything. She'd been born and raised in these mountains and it was her home. Over the years, she'd seen many outsiders come and go, but she'd never seen one as intensely stressed-out as the sandy-haired man wearing a gray silk Armani suit in the muggy summer weather.

Two weeks.

He'd been at Bosque de Los Dioses for two weeks and she had never once seen him in blue jeans or shorts or sandals or even a short-sleeved shirt. Always the suit and tie and expensive leather shoes as if he was in a New York City boardroom instead of a tropical paradise.

Why?

The question fascinated her. *He* fascinated her.

She dipped the brim of her well-worn straw cowgirl hat, the band decorated with a purple orchid that she'd plucked from a nearby vine. And pushed her heart-shaped pink sunglasses up on her nose to study him through the rose-tinged lenses.

Hombre guapo.

He paced the length of the veranda of the luxury tree house bungalow nestled in the tops of the Flame of the Forest and Ron-Ron trees, a cell phone pressed to his ear. The sunlight reflected off the thick platinum link chain bracelet at his broad wrist. The bracelet was like the rest of him, polished, sleek but underneath the shiny exterior undeniably masculine.

Although she had not asked, he was clearly a wealthy businessman, brash, entitled and constantly in motion. Who else rushed, rushed, rushed to get to the same place everyone else was going?

"Eventually, no matter where you are from, you end up in the graveyard," her father often said. "Might as well take your time getting there and enjoy the view."

That was the Costa Rican way—slow and easy and grateful for what you had. Then again, no other country had views like this. Perhaps it was easier to be philosophical when surrounded by so much beauty.

And speaking of views…

This one was as delicious as el casado.

No, maybe not el casado since it meant "married" in Spanish because the meal was the perfect marriage

of beans, rice, fried plantains, salad and some kind of
meat. Traditionally, it was the noon meal and had been
named for the fact it was the usual food wives packed
for their husbands to brown bag to work. This man
looked as far from an attentive husband as he could
get and the thought of him brown bagging anything
made her chuckle.

Sunlight glinted off his golden hair cut short in a
neat style that flattered his features—firm chin, but
not big-jawed. If it hadn't been for the broken nose he
might have been too pretty and Sophia had to admit
she had a thing for blonds. Growing up around so many
dark-haired men had given her a sharp appreciation for
flaxen locks.

Mmm. She licked her lips.

His name, according to the credit card he'd used to
pay for his flight, was Gibb Martin. He was close to
six feet tall and moved with the sleek grace of a jaguar,
lean and athletic, as if his skin could barely contain his
excessive masculine energy. She imagined running her
hands over his biceps and her palms tingled.

Although she couldn't see them from here, Sophia
knew he possessed piercing, no-nonsense gray eyes,
that when they were directed at her, made her feel as if
he could see straight into her soul.

Sophia shivered.

He'd caught her with those eyes the day she'd flown
him in from the Libera Airport. He'd thanked her for
the flight, shook her hand and held it for just a moment
too long. Her heart had skipped a beat and she couldn't
help feeling that it was a watershed moment.

Or maybe that had all been in her imagination.

He'd had a woman with him after all. A tall, skinny

blonde with pouty lips, pixie haircut and breasts the
size of pillows, quite a contrast to Sophia's own short
stature, well rounded hips, waist-length black hair and
rather modest endowments. When she was a teenager,
her brothers had teasingly called her *Tortita,* the Spanish word for pancake. Luckily, she'd sprouted a bit since
then, but not much.

The blonde had not seemed happy. She'd complained
about everything—the smallness of the plane, the sticky
humidity and the fact that the cookies and crackers that
Sophia kept onboard for guests were not gluten-free.
Then again, in the blonde's defense, the American had
barely looked up from his laptop computer the entire
flight and she ended up feeling sorry for her.

Two weeks had passed and the blonde still wasn't
happy. She came out on the balcony, hands sunk onto
her hips, rocking a red G-string bikini so small it could
have doubled as a pair of shoelaces.

Frump. Compared to a woman like that, Sophia was
a dumpy dowager in cutoff blue jeans and a white crop
top.

"Gibby!" Blondie yelled at him.

He frowned in irritation, motioned at the phone, gave
her a hush-this-is-an-important-call glower.

Poor Blondie. He had no time for his gorgeous girlfriend.

The blonde scowled. "If you don't get off the damn
phone and take me somewhere fun I'm flying back to
Miami tonight."

He pressed the phone against his chest, stepped close
to whisper something to her and then playfully swatted her bottom.

Blondie giggled.

Something in Sophia's mouth tasted as bad as a green plantain. Jealous much?

Jealous? Of course not. Why would she be jealous of a drop-dead model with million mile legs who had a rich, handsome man on a string? A handsome man who ignored her most of the time. Sophia would never settle for that. She would demand burning passion.

Blondie held out her palm and looked sheepish.

He fished in his back pocket for his wallet and from where Sophia was laying it looked like he pulled out an American Express black card and dropped it into her palm. The blonde closed her fingers around the card, leaned over and kissed his cheek.

Buying her off.

Sophia snorted. How could she be jealous of *that?*

Since his arrival, Gibb Martin had either been on the phone or in meetings with the cadre of other businessmen that Sophia had flown in, while the blonde had spent her time at the Bosque de Los Dioses luxury spa.

Sophia's oldest sister, Josephina, worked at the spa as a massage therapist. In order to work for or contract with Bosque de Los Dioses you had to sign a confidentially agreement; they could only gossip about the clientele with each other and even then they had to make sure no one overheard their conversations.

A few minutes later, Josie came out of the employee entrance, toting her own brown bag casado. *"Hola."*

"What's up?"

Although they had been raised in a bilingual household, Josie preferred to speak Spanish, while Sophia thought of English words before the Spanish equivalent popped in her mind. Probably because she'd lived with her aunt in California the year after their mother had died and being so young, she'd had no trouble adapting to that culture. Sophia set the hammock to rocking by pushing against the palm tree with her big toe.

"Nothing new." Josie plunked down on the cement bench beside the rows of empty hammocks strung from the trees for the guests to enjoy. At this time of the afternoon almost everyone was out on an excursion. "How about you?"

"Waiting to take a fare to Libera at two."

"How is El Diablo holding up these days? That plane is as old as I am." Josie was forty-one, fourteen years older than Sophia and she'd been married to her high school sweetheart, Jorge, for more than half her life. They had three children who were high school age.

"I've got the plane running like a top."

El Diablo was the contrary 1971 Piper Cherokee 180F she'd inherited from their father after he'd retired two years ago. She was the only one of the seven Cruz offspring who'd had any interest in flying.

No one had begrudged her the gift of the plane. Her siblings considered the plane a burden, not a blessing, and granted it was something of a heap, but it was how she made her living. Flying tourists into the Cloud Forest where only bush planes could go. She dearly loved flying and had just finished aircraft maintenance school so she could keep El Diablo in the best flying condition possible.

Josie unwrapped homemade beef tamales from the plantain leaf they had been cooked in. "You've made Poppy very proud."

Sophia sneaked another glance at Gibb Martin's tree house bungalow. Blondie had come out on the veranda and was leaning against the balcony railing. The woman waved at her sister Josie and smiled.

Josie waved and smiled back.

"You know her?"

"Every day on my massage table for the last two weeks. She's *my* two o'clock appointment and she tips big with her boyfriend's credit card. I will smile and wave at her all day if that's what she wants."

"She seems a bit superficial." Okay, that was snide. Contrite, Sophia popped three fingers over her mouth.

"Stacy is a cover model," Josie said. "What else would you expect from her?"

"Something a bit less cliché?"

"Does your prickly tongue have anything to do with the fact that she's the girlfriend of that handsome American venture capitalist you keep staring at?"

"I do not stare at him."

"Uh-huh."

"Well, maybe a little, but how often do you see blond men around here? It's not him personally. It's just his hair."

"Uh-huh."

"It is."

Josie nodded at an overweight bald guy in his thirties who was horsing around with his buddies on one of the rope footbridges that linked the bungalows to the main lodge. "You are telling me that you would stare at that man if he had blond hair?"

"Yes, sure," she lied.

Josie snorted. "By the way, the venture capitalist stares back at you too when you're not looking."

"He does?" she asked, surprised to hear her voice come out an octave higher.

Josie nodded. "He stares hard."

Sophia gulped, ducked her head, and felt heat flush her cheeks. Hey, what was this? She wasn't a blushy-gushy kind of girl.

Josie sent her a knowing glance. "Things are not going well with Emilio?"

"What?" Sophia startled. "No. Emilio is great—"

"But Emilio is in San Jose and Mr. Tall, Blond and Handsome is here?"

"I didn't say that."

"You didn't have to."

Her sister was wrong. She wasn't that fickle. Was she?

"Sophia," Josie wheedled. "You can tell me. What is it?"

Sophia shrugged. The bark on the palm tree at the end of the hammock had sloughed off from where the ropes had rubbed it. "It's nothing really."

Josie clucked her tongue, shook her head. Sophia had never been able to keep anything from her older sister.

"Emilio and I are sliding more toward solid friend-ship than red-hot romance," she admitted. "We have not even made love yet."

"But you've been dating what, two months?"

"My point exactly. Only five dates in two months. If this relationship was headed somewhere important, should we not pine for each other every time we are apart? Am I wrong?"

"You expect too much," Josie said. "Emilio is a nice man. He would make a good husband and father."

"And that's enough?"

Josie gave a knowing smile, dusted crumbs from her fingers and got to her feet. "What else is there?"

"Passion for one thing."

"Passion fades. That's when friendship counts."

"You make marriage sound so boring." Sophia yawned.

"Not at all. As time goes on, you will learn to value other things above passion."

"That might work for you," she said. "But me? I want sparks. All the time. Fireworks or nothing."

Josie made a quiet chiding noise. "You're more like Mother than you think. You've got her starry-eyed idealism."

"There's nothing wrong with setting my standards high."

"There is having high standards and then there are unrealistic expectations."

"If Mother hadn't believed in passionate love that lasted she wouldn't have stayed in Costa Rica and had seven children."

"True, but look at everything she gave up."

"For *love*."

"It wasn't easy for her. Starting over in a new country. Learning another language. Navigating a strange culture."

"But she did it because she loved Poppy so much. That's what I want. Someone who'd swim the deepest ocean for me."

"You're not going to start singing are you?"

"I might," Sophia teased, splayed a hand to her chest and sang an off key rendition of "I'd Climb the Highest Mountain," except she didn't know most of the words and ended up stumble-humming it.

"You are not getting any younger, *mi hija*. Soon your best child-bearing years will be behind you."

"Thanks for that." Sophia crossed her legs. The orchid slid off the brim of her hat, landed on her nose. Sophia brushed it aside.

"You can't keep hitting the snooze button on your biological clock." Josie pressed her lips into a disapproving line.

"I'm not even remotely thinking of babies yet."

"I know, but you should be."

"I'm not done having fun yet."

"Babies are a different kind of fun."

"Uh-huh. If you say so."

"You love your nieces and nephews."

"I do. Stop trying to sell me on motherhood. When I find the right relationship—packed with tons of passion—the rest will take care of itself." Sophia's eyes were on the hombre who was going to pace a hole right through the wooden planks of the balcony.

Josie canted her head. "The American isn't right for you."

"Of course he's not. I never thought he was. He's caviar and I'm black beans, but a girl needs her sexual fantasies, right?"

"Give Emilio a chance," Josie advised and picked up her sandwich bag. "Bring him to Sunday dinner."

"We'll see."

Josie pointed a finger at her. "Just bring him."

Sophia rolled her eyes. Their mother had died of bacterial meningitis when Sophia was twelve and after Sophia had returned from living in California with Aunt Kristi, Josie had taken over as Mother Hen and sometimes she could be a bit overbearing. *"Sí."*

"I mean it."

Sophia made shooing motions at her. "Go back to rubbing that rich cover model's backside."

"I love you," Josie said sweetly over her shoulder.

"You're not going to make me feel like a brat."

"Even if you are being one?" Josie laughed and went into the spa.

Sophia pursed her lips and looked back to Gibb Martin's bungalow. Blondie was gone, but he was still pacing and talking on the phone.

Did the man ever slow down? Take a deep breath? Relax? Enjoy himself for half a second?

She shifted her gaze to the sky and estimated the time by the sun's position. She never wore a watch. Two o'clock was perhaps thirty minutes away. Just enough time to fuel the plane and do her flight checks. Yawning, she rolled out of the hammock and stretched big, reaching for the clouds, her crop top rising up high with her movements.

Gibb Martin leaned over the railing of his balcony.

He was watching her!

Her stomach churned and she had the strangest feeling that something monumental was about to happen.

Those compelling gray eyes stared straight at her. Thank God for her sunglasses.

A slow smile slid across his face.

Excitement shot through her and she suppressed a smug grin. He might not be paying Miss Cover Model much attention, but he was certainly focused on *her*.

What she did next wasn't noble, but it was human. She pretended she hadn't seen him watching her. She swept off her cowgirl hat, tilted her head back, and ran her fingers through her long hair, fluffing it up in a sexy, just-rolled out of bed style and bit down on her bottom lip to make it puffy.

Bad girl, bad. *Mala. Mala.*

She strolled away, emphasizing each sway of her hips, and headed for the plane. Was that the heat of his gaze she felt on her shoulders?

Casually, she turned, looked up at the balcony, only to find it empty.

Her face flamed hot as she realized she'd strutted for an audience of no one.

Idiot.

Never mind. It didn't matter. It wasn't even a flirtation. That's how limited their exchanges had been, a few furtive glances, a handshake that lingered a bit too long, that's all there was to it.

But the fact that she was fantasizing about a good-looking stranger who had a cover model girlfriend told Sophia that this thing with Emilio simply wasn't working for her. They would be better off as friends.

It was time to tell him that.

After work, she had planned to fly to San Jose for a cookout with Emilio. In spite of the provisions she'd packed in an Igloo cooler this morning, she would forego the cookout, sit him down and make it perfectly clear she wanted nothing more than friendship from him.

Was she stupid for cutting loose a good guy who would make a wonderful husband? Maybe. But something told her that she did not have to settle. Somewhere out there was a good man who would also ignite passion in her heart and she wasn't going to stop looking until she found him.

2

THROUGH THE OPEN wooden slats of the bamboo blinds, Gibb watched the sexy little bush pilot's butt bounce. He shouldn't be looking. He was here with Stacy after all, but there was something about the sultry Costa Rican that had captured him from the minute he'd laid eyes on her in Libera Airport.

And this thing with Stacy had just about run its course. Two years was already eighteen months longer than he'd anticipated it would last. Both of them had known from the beginning it wasn't a long-term relationship. He required a poised, beautiful woman on his arm to take to business functions and she had wanted someone with an unlimited expense account.

They'd met each other's needs at the time, but now they were starting to get on each other's nerves. Stacy continually accused him of being a workaholic—hey, how did she think he paid for her shopping sprees?—and he'd wearied of her constant bid for his attention. Bringing Stacy with him to Bosque de Los Dioses had been a mistake and not just because he wanted to flirt with the pilot.

She was examining her plane, doing a preflight check, and as she reached up to inspect the flaps, her white crop top moved up to expose even more of her smooth, tanned skin. Sunlight glimmered off her gold navel ring and her long black hair swung just above the curve of her back.

Gibb gulped. She curved in all the right places. The white cotton top stretched over breasts the size of perfectly ripe peaches. His mouth watered instantly.

She wore cutoff blue jean shorts with frayed threads dangling down her firm thighs. The pink straw cowgirl hat was tipped back on her head, and the matching pink heart-shaped sunglasses slid halfway down her pert little nose. The woman had a thing for pink. On the flight in, she'd smelled of delicious pink grapefruit, fresh, clean and tartly sweet.

What did she have on beneath those jeans? Pink boy shorts? A pink thong? Maybe nothing at all?

His body heated all over.

Hang on there, Martin. He might not be a long-term commitment kind of guy, but when he was in a relationship—no matter how casual—he didn't mess around.

"You're a serial monogamist," his best friend Coast Guard Lieutenant Scott Everly often teased. It was true, he never dated more than one woman at a time.

Gibb's cell phone rang.

He stepped back from the window, pulled the phone from his pocket and looked at the caller ID.

Speak of the devil.

Scott had been dodging his calls of late and Gibb wondered if it was because his buddy was having second thoughts about leaving the Coast Guard. He and Scott were going into business together on this clandestine, environmentally green project that promised to revolutionize the way people traveled.

That was what Gibb was doing here in Cordillera of Tilarán. The planning stage was finally complete. And although the patent was still pending, it was only a matter of time until it was granted. He had complete confidence in that. The inventor would be arriving next week. It was time to start building the prototype track for the breakthrough monorail system that would extend the thirty miles from Bosque de Los Dioses to Monteverde.

Building the prototype track here would serve two purposes. One, it would eventually make Bosque de Los Dioses accessible by some other mode of transportation besides bush plane. And two, the remote location and thick vegetation discouraged the corporate spies that had dogged him. Twice in the last two years, spies from Fisby Corp had burned him by stealing the ideas he'd invested in and getting them to market before he did. He wasn't going to allow that to happen again.

That's where Scott was to come in. He was the only one Gibb trusted to handle his private security. They'd been talking about partnering up for the past two years, ever since Gibb had first invested in this project. They'd just been waiting for Scott's commission with the Coast Guard to be over to get started on it. Waiting, however, was making Gibb antsy. The longer it took, the more likely it was that someone would rip off the idea before the patent was granted.

Gibb hit the talk button. "Guy, where have you been?"

"Falling in love," Scott replied.

Gibb laughed. "So when are you getting out of the

Coast Guard? How long before you can get to Costa Rica? I need you here."

"I'm serious," Scott said. "I've fallen in love with the most amazing woman. She's smart and sexy and—"

Gibb snorted. "Stop pulling my leg. We're ready to hit the ground running. I have to tell you that arranging to have supplies delivered up here, while trying to keep things tightly under wraps has been nothing short of a logistical nightmare."

"You're not listening to me."

"Sure I am, you're madly in love. Good. Great. Congrats. Now when can I expect you?"

"She's the daughter of Jack Birchard, the renowned oceanographer, but Jackie is a damn fine oceanographer in her own right," Scott went on as if he hadn't said a thing.

Gibb scratched his head. "You're serious?"

"I'm stone cold in love, buddy."

"Okay." Gibb plowed fingers through his hair, tried not to fret. "What does Jackie think about you living in Costa Rica for a couple of years?"

"I'm not leaving the Coast Guard."

"C'mon. We've talked about this forever. I can't do it without you."

"Sure you can."

"All right, I don't want to do it without you. This project has the potential to make us billionaires."

"You're already a billionaire, Gibb."

"Not now I'm not. Not after all I've got invested in this technology."

"Aw, so now you're only a multi-millionaire? How will you ever survive?"

"Scott, I can't believe you're doing this to me. Remember when we were kids, camping out in a tent in your parents' backyard? Even then we talked about working together someday, but you had to go off and join the Coast Guard."

"You were supposed to join with me," Scott reminded him.

"Is it my fault that I get seasick?"

Joining the Coast Guard was the best thing Gibb had never done. If he had joined the Coast Guard, he wouldn't have invented a popular gaming app that had made him a multi-millionaire and started him on the road to becoming a venture capitalist, investing in other people's ideas.

He had a knack for spotting trends before they took off and it paid big dividends. Charismatic forward thinker, *Wealth Maker Magazine* had called him. Unfortunately, that had made him a target for the unscrupulous looking to get in on his action. Forcing Gibb to become even more secretive and suspicious of others than he already was. Scott was the one person in the whole wide world that he trusted with his life.

"No, just like it's not my fault that I fell in love."

"You're leaving me hanging?"

"I'm sorry, Gibb, but I've found something more. I don't want to end up like you."

Two whips of hurt and anger lashed through him. "What's that supposed to mean?"

"I don't want to be consumed by work the way you are."

An accusing silence stretched over the miles between them.

"If I wasn't consumed by work, I wouldn't be where I am today," he said.

"Where are you, Gibb?"

"At the top of the freaking world."

"Alone."

"I'm not alone. I have a cover model girlfriend and my Bentley and my beach house and—"

"I'm getting married on Saturday in Key West on the Fourth of July, aboard the *Sea Anemone,* Wharf 16 at 4:00 p.m. I hope you'll be there."

It wasn't until this very moment that Gibb understood exactly how much he'd been looking forward to not only working with Scott, but bringing him in on this deal. It was Gibb's way of paying his buddy back for the time Scott had literally saved his life.

Gibb pushed the platinum bracelet up on his wrist. Scott had a matching bracelet. They'd bought the man jewelry together, a symbol of their brotherhood and undying friendship after that crazy diving trip to the Great Barrier Reef where Gibb had been barbed in the chest by a stingray. Only Scott's quick action and first aid training had prevented Gibb from removing the barb. He'd come within seconds of ending up like the famous crocodile hunter, Steve Irwin.

Reflexively, Gibb rubbed his chest. "*This* Saturday?"

"This Saturday."

"But it's Wednesday!"

"I know."

"Why didn't you tell me sooner?"

"Because Jackie and I just got engaged."

"What? Why so fast?"

"When it's right, it's right. We can't wait any longer to be together."

"So she's pregnant."

"No, she's not pregnant." Scott sounded irritated.

"Whoa, back up the truck. I talked to you six weeks ago and you didn't say a word about this Jackie woman. How long have you known her?"

"A month," Scott confessed, not sounding the least bit sheepish.

"A month! You're marrying someone you've only known a month?"

"Don't rain on my parade. She's the love of my life," Scott growled.

Taken aback, Gibb blinked. He couldn't believe this was his childhood buddy. "I recall you saying a time or two that you were never getting married."

"Dumb. That was back when I was dumb and stupid. I'd never been in love before. I never knew it could feel like this."

"I recall you once said the same thing about that waitress in Panama." Who in the hell was this woman who'd woven such a spell over Scott?

"That was lust. There's a big difference. I know that now. You'll know it too when you find it."

Gibb frowned. "Hang on, this too will pass."

"No. No, it won't." Scott sounded adamant.

"You say that now—"

Scott cut him off. "Can we expect to see you at the wedding?"

"There shouldn't be a wedding. You're throwing away all our plans, and re-upping in the Coast Guard when you'd planned to get out and—"

"Sorry, but meeting Jackie has changed everything."

"I get that. It's what scares me."

"Come to the wedding if you want, but you're not changing my mind."

"This is craziness!" Gibb yanked at the knot of his tie. "You've lost your mind over a piece of—"

"Don't say it," Scott threatened.

Gibb was so upset that he couldn't stop himself from saying it. "Tail."

A dial tone sounded in his ear.

His very best buddy on the planet had just hung up on him. Shocked, Gibb stared at the phone. Disturbing how fate could turn life on a whim.

SOPHIA WAS FILLING up the gas tank on El Diablo when Gibb Martin came stalking up to her, his eyes narrowed, his jaw tight and a determined expression on his lips.

"I need you to fly me to Key West, Florida," he demanded.

She cocked an eyebrow at him, holstered the nozzle back into the pump. "What bit you?"

"I want to leave right now." He tapped the face of his Rolex with an impatient finger.

"Mosquito? Botfly? Hornet?"

If he were a cartoon, steam would be shooting out of his ears. "No joking around. Time is of the essence."

She lifted one shoulder. "Sorry, amigo."

"I'll pay handsomely."

"No can do."

"What?" He looked stunned that she'd refused him. "N.O. Nada."

"How much would it take to change your mind?"

"Money is not the issue."

"What is?"

"Well, for one thing, I already have a 2:00 p.m. fare."

"They can wait. Call another bush pilot."

What an arrogant tool he was. "My, we have a grand sense of our own importance, don't we?"

Gibb snorted, pressing his lips into a firm line. "This is an emergency."

"An emergency?" That changed everything. Why was she such a smart mouth? "Oh, I'm so sorry," she said contritely. "Did someone die?"

"Worse."

Sophia put a hand to her heart. "What is worse than death?"

"Marriage."

Confused, Sophia pushed her hat back on her head. "Someone is getting married? That is your emergency?"

"Yes." His voice was flat, brooking no more questions.

Sophia questioned anyway. "You're against marriage?"

"Not in general. Not for most people. It's just not my personal bailiwick."

"Bailiwick?"

"It means sphere of knowledge."

She grimaced. "Fan-*cy*."

"Once upon a time I hired a vocabulary coach, deal with it."

She raised both palms. "Communication doesn't work unless you can speak so that others understand you."

"Andalé, andalé." He made shooing motions at her. "How's that for communication?"

"Have you been watching old Speedy Gonzales cartoons?"

"It's not the correct word?" His face colored.

"Not if you don't mind sounding like a cartoon

mouse. *Vámonos* or *rápido* might be what you're looking for."

"Well, let's *vámonos, rápido, rápido*."

"There's one thing I'm still unclear on."

He exhaled loudly. "What's that?"

"How is marriage an emergency?"

"I have to stop the wedding."

"Ah, I see." She nodded.

"See what?"

"You are still hung up on a former lover and she has broken your heart by marrying another before you could reconcile."

"No, no." He shifted, jammed his hands in his pockets and leaned in closer to her. "That's not it at all."

She caught a whiff of his scent—kumquat, leather, musk—nice cologne. "Then what *is* it?"

"She's all wrong for him."

"Who?"

"He has only known her a month," Gibb muttered.

"Who?"

"It's ridiculous."

"Why?"

"A month!" Gibb exclaimed. "My best friend is getting married to a woman that he's only known for one month."

"Oh, I see. That clearly is the end of the world."

"Would *you* marry a man you'd only known for a month?"

Sophia grinned, trying to get him to lighten up. "Depends on the man."

He scoffed, "Don't tell me you're one of those."

"One of what?"

"Die-hard romantics."

"I have not found my true love but that doesn't mean I don't believe he's not out there somewhere."

Gibb raised his face to the sky. "Please, spare me the love impaired."

"What is wrong with love?"

"It muddles the brain. Clouds your judgment. Makes you do dumb things like get married to someone you've only known a month."

"But what if this woman makes your friend truly happy?"

"She doesn't. He just thinks she does."

"How do you know that for sure?"

"Look, I don't have time to stand around here dissecting it to death. My best buddy is about to make the biggest mistake of his life. I have to leave immediately for Key West to save him from himself."

"You can't tell him this over the telephone?"

"He hung up on me." Gibb sounded highly offended. "And when I tried to call him back, he wouldn't answer and he's disabled his voicemail."

"I can see why. Clearly, you are overreacting."

He held up both palms. "Look, I don't need your opinion. I just need your flying expertise. How much would you charge to fly me to Key West right now?"

Sophia cast a glance over her shoulder at El Diablo. She'd never flown any farther than Belize. "My plane is not equipped to fly such a long distance. It's over fifteen hundred kilometers to Key West."

He waved a hand. "You can do it. I've watched you fly passengers in and out for the last two weeks. You're an excellent pilot."

He had been watching her? Sophia's cheeks warmed. His flattery was dangerous. Damn this desire to show off her piloting skills and prove him right. "Thank you very much for the compliment, but the gas tanks on a plane this size only hold so much fuel. We would have to stop to refuel."

"So we stop. Let's go." He opened the pilot's door of the plane and motioned for her to hop in.

She stepped over to shut the door. "You are a very annoying man."

"How much?" He took out his wallet, started pulling out several one-hundred-dollar bills. "Two thousand do it?"

Sophia blinked. Two thousand dollars? That would pay off her debt from mechanic school. "You will pay for the fuel, as well?"

"Yes, absolutely."

"You are a desperate man."

"Yes, yes, I am. I'm also a rich one and I always get what I want."

"Not this time." Sophia folded her arms over her chest. "On top of everything else, there is a tropical depression brewing in the Caribbean."

"It could easily go way north of Florida."

"Perhaps. Perhaps not."

"When is it expected to hit landfall?"

She shrugged. "Weather is unpredictable, two days, maybe."

"Two days?" he blurted. "We will be in Key West long before that."

"The storm could hit sooner," she said, arguing with herself as much as with him.

"Or later."

"True."

"It might even dissipate altogether."

"I am not in the habit of gambling with the lives of my passengers."

"Look," he said. "You can check the weather along the way, if the storm moves faster than expected I'll admit defeat and take it as a sign that Scott and Jackie are meant to be."

"Can you accept that?"

"You're the pilot. Once we're in the air, you're in control of that plane."

Hmm, interesting admission for someone who seemed to be something of a control freak. Could she trust him to keep his word? "It's not as simple as jumping into the plane and taking off. I'll have to make a flight plan, get permission to fly into the airspace of the other countries along the way."

He had run out of cash, but he was now tugging out a plethora of credit cards. "Three thousand."

Sophia moistened her lips. How high was he willing to go?

Lunacy. It was sheer lunacy to even consider flying him to Florida, but the part of her that loved a challenge *wanted* to give it a go. See if she could do it. If nothing else, she would learn what she and El Diablo were really made of.

Priorities, Sophia.

It was a lesson her mother had repeated to her often. She did have a tendency to put adventure ahead of responsibility. Besides, she was supposed to go over to Emilio's house for a cookout tonight. In fact, this was the night she'd decided to have "the talk" with him. Then again, what would it hurt to delay breaking bad news?

"Mr. Martin, I will happily fly you to Libera with

my current passengers and there you can catch the next plane to Florida," she offered.

He looked uneasy. "That solution doesn't work for me."

"Why not?" Puzzled, she canted her head, studied him intently.

"I do not have to explain myself to you."

"You don't have your own jet? A rich man like you?"

"I do have my own jet, but that's none of your business."

"Oh," she said. "I get it. You don't want anyone tracking your whereabouts."

He seemed relieved. "Yes. Your discretion in this matter is very important to me. Can I trust you?"

"Of course." If she couldn't keep a secret she would have been out of a job a long time ago. Her sister Josie was the only person she could confide in about such things.

The couple from Argentina that she was supposed to fly to Libera arrived at the plane. A bellhop in a golf cart with their bags in the back followed behind the couple.

"Here are my passengers, Mr. Martin. I'm sorry about your dilemma but—"

Gibb pivoted on his heel to face the male passenger, a distinguished-looking gray-haired man in his mid-fifties. "How much for you to take another bush plane to the airport?"

"Pardon, *señor?*" the man asked.

Gibb waved the cash at him. "How much? I need this plane."

"You are not thinking rationally, Mr. Martin," Sophia pointed out. It surprised her that the cool blond American could be so filled with passion. To the couple, she said, "He is trying to stop a wedding."

"Ah, *amor*," said the woman. "Isn't that romantic? He wants to claim his woman before she marries someone else."

Sophia noticed that Gibb did not bother to correct the woman's erroneous assumption.

The Argentinean wasn't losing out on the opportunity. He plucked the bills from Gibb's hand and tucked into his pocket. "The plane is all yours, *señor*." He put an arm around his wife's waist. "How can we stand in the way of true love?"

"You're willingly giving up your seats? You could miss your connecting flight while waiting on another bush plane to arrive."

"We are flying standby," the Argentinean said. "If we miss one flight…" He shrugged. "We'll catch another."

The bellhop gave them a ride back to the lodge in the golf cart.

Gibb held out both arms. "Problem solved. Let's hit the road, Amelia."

"My name is Sophia. Sophia Cruz."

"Amelia Earhart reference not doing it? I thought every woman pilot loved to be compared to Amelia."

"That's presumptive and sexist. See, I know big words, too."

"So you don't like Amelia Earhart?"

"You did not remember my name, did you?"

"So I forgot your name," he admitted sheepishly. "Sorry."

"My dog apologizes better than that." Okay, so she was stretching the truth a bit. Her dog died last year.

Her heart twinged at the thought of Trixie. She'd had her for fourteen years and missed her deeply.

"Dogs are all about apology. Which is why I don't have one."

"Why? Because you hate creatures who have more love in their little toe than you do in your entire body."

"No," he said. "I actually love dogs, but I'm never home and I'd have to apologize to the poor thing for hiring someone to take care of it and then I'd feel guilty. Well, you see where I'm going with this."

"Not really."

"Doesn't matter. Can we do this thing?"

She should say no. The sensible thing would be to say no. Most anyone else would say no. He was pushy and arrogant and exasperating, but at the same time, a thrill ran through her at the thought of flying all the way to Florida. Still, was it prudent? Only one person could tell her if it was worth the risk, if indeed El Diablo could make the long trip. She'd have to ask her father.

Gibb was already climbing into the plane.

"Not so fast, *Norte,*" she said.

One eyebrow shot up on his forehead and the opposite corner of his mouth quirked up at the same time. *"Norte?"*

"*Norte* means someone who comes from the north, usually from the U.S.A. Isn't that what you are?"

"The way you said it, it sounds derogative."

"No." She slowly shook her head. "That is all on you. If you think that being from the U.S.A. is derogative, that's your belief system not mine."

He stood straighter, stiffened his back. "I do not believe that it's a bad thing to be from the U.S."

"Neither do I, so why are you taking offense at the word *Norte?*" she asked.

He pointed at her. A slow smile crept across his face. "You're a sly one, Ms. Cruz."

She feigned an affronted expression. "I don't know what you mean."

"You're messing with my head."

"If you did not have a chip on your shoulder, I could not knock it off."

"Can we just get this show on the road?"

"Before I agree to this arrangement, I must first make some phone calls."

He tapped his wrist. "Time's wasting."

"That's a bracelet, not a watch."

"All the same, you get the sentiment. It's the universal sign for hurry up."

"Norte," she muttered.

"That time you *were* being derogatory."

"You're sort of a jackass, you know that?"

He clenched his determined jaw. "It doesn't matter as long as I get what I want."

Now she was beginning to understand why Blondie looked annoyed ninety percent of the time, but Sophia certainly understood the push-pull attraction to Gibb Martin. While part of her wanted to throttle him, another part of her wanted to kiss him.

All the more reason for her not to take him to Key West.

So why did she agree?

3

GIBB PACED OUTSIDE THE plane and repeatedly checked his watch. *C'mon, C'mon.* He didn't have all day. He tried several times to call Scott while Sophia was pre-occupied, but his buddy was still not picking up. *Hey, can you blame him? You acted like a jerk.*

For Scott's own good!

They had known each other since they first swapped sandwiches on the kindergarten playground. Gibb had readily pawned off his lobster roll for Scott's plain old peanut butter and grape jelly sammie. Scott had taken one bite of the lobster roll and started crying and demanded to swap back. They laughed about it now. How dumb they'd both been to prefer PB and J to lobster. How clueless Gibb's mother had been about the appropriate lunch for a five-year-old.

That was Gibb's mother all the way. Winnie had exquisite luxury tastes and assumed everyone else did, too, even though when he was growing up, they'd had a beer budget that did not match with her champagne thirst.

On more than one occasion, the cops had come to

their front door to tell her she had to make restitution on bounced checks or she would end up in jail. Somehow, she'd always manage to skirt the law until she hit the jackpot by marrying Florida real estate mogul, James Martin, who legally adopted Gibb when he was seven. And Gibb had been trying to prove himself worthy of James's largesse ever since.

"It is settled."

The smell of plumeria, sweet and exotic, wafted over him and he looked up to see Sophia. The woman possessed gorgeous brown eyes with impossibly long dark lashes. A hot tug of attraction pulled at him.

"Settled yes or settled no?" he asked.

"For three thousand dollars, plus you pay the price of fuel, I will fly you to Key West."

He had thought for sure she was going to say no and he would have to risk hiring a jet in Libera and pray the spies weren't that close. He'd gone through all kinds of machinations to get to Bosque de Los Dioses. First by buying two airline tickets to Europe that had gone unused for him and Stacy. Then hiring a small private plane to Nicaragua, checking into a low-rent motel in San Carlos under an assumed name, and from there hired a car to drive them to Libera. He thought he'd adequately covered his tracks. But, if any of his competitors found out he was in Costa Rica, well, two years' worth of work and a hundred million dollars would be shot all to hell.

"Hot damn. Let's go."

"Will your companion be joining us?" Sophia asked.

"Who?" he asked, and then realized she was talking about Stacy. "No. She's got spa treatments and whatnot to keep her occupied while I'm gone."

"Do you have luggage?"

"No time. Don't need any."

"Don't you at least want to change?" She waved at his business suit.

"I'm good. Let's hit it."

Sophia held out her palm. "I will require payment up front."

He handed over a credit card, and couldn't help noticing what pretty hands she had. Long, slender fingers, nails painted a soft salmon color. It was unusual for a petite woman to have such long fingers.

"I will be right back." She trotted off again, headed toward the airport's employee entrance.

His palms were unexpectedly sweaty and his knees felt slightly shaky. Was he that nervous she would turn him down? Or was he simply amped up over Scott's crazy news? Either way, the shakiness was disconcerting. Why did he care so much about what Scott decided to do with his life?

Sophia returned a few minutes later with his credit card and a sunny smile.

He pocketed his card. "Now can we leave?"

"Almost. I must finish my flight check first."

Gibb got into the passenger seat and impatiently drummed his fingers against the dashboard as she went through the checklist. He kept thinking of Scott and his project and how if he couldn't talk his buddy out of marriage it was going to upend all his plans.

Sophia climbed into the cockpit, doffed her pink cowgirl hat, tossed it in the back and donned a headset. She communicated with the airport in Libera and a few minutes later they were rolling down the narrow dirt landing strip. Just when it seemed they were about to run out of road and fall off the mountain plateau, the plane was smoothly airborne and they were flying through a thick white mist.

The resort was at five thousand feet. Gibb knew small planes like this one maxed out at ten thousand feet, but Sophia didn't even take them that high. She leveled off their ascent so they were just skimming over the cloud-shrouded mountain range.

It was a mystical sight—the smoky clouds, wafting lazily around them, parting here and there to reveal shades of deep tropical green or craggy blue-gray rock formations. The view took his breath away.

Sophia sat relaxed in the seat, her dark hair curling sexy tendrils around her face, an otherworldly smile on her full pink lips, her hands loose on the yoke. The pink-and-white V-neck quarter-length T-shirt that she wore clung snuggly to her smallish but firm breasts. Tanned, shapely legs worked pedals on the floor that controlled the rudders.

He moved his left arm at the same time she moved her right, and their elbows bumped. A staggering streak of lust shot from his elbow to his shoulder and arrowed straight down to his groin. Instantly, he jerked his arm away.

So did she.

"Sorry," he mumbled, his heart punching hard against his chest.

The seats in a plane this small were disturbingly close. He should have sat in the back. Why hadn't he sat in the back?

Sophia stared intently out the windshield. She had a delicate profile—a diminutive nose, gently sloped forehead, small but well-formed chin—that complimented her petite stature. Not a complex face that an artist might find a challenge to sketch, but a fun face, an open face, a happy face.

Looking at her made him smile. He did not want to smile.

There was no swelling of peppy music, no Ferris Bueller, "Oh Yeah" deep-based chorus, but the feeling that his life was about to change and change big, dug into Gibb and clung tight.

She guided the plane with what seemed to be an innate ease. Gibb had never thought of flying as anything more than a skill that anyone who put their mind to it could learn, but right now, watching her, his old belief disappeared, replaced by a deep certainty that there was such a think as a natural born pilot. She had an effortless, light touch on the controls and her sense of timing was impeccable. It was as if she'd strapped the airplane onto her, the way an old west gunslinger strapped on a holster, and the plane started to *breathe* with her.

Something told him he would relive this moment again in his dreams—the point where the cocky cowgirl became the consummate aviatrix and she was transformed. He felt transformed just by sitting next to her. He would be able to lie in bed at night, close his eyes and be with her again on wings of air, floating into a sweet, deep peace. If he could eat this moment, it would taste like one perfect bite of amazing amuse-bouclé— bitter, sweet, salty, sour, savory, piquant.

"I never tire of the beauty." Sophia breathed.

"Impressive." Gibb didn't take his eyes off her.

She turned her head, caught him staring. Her smile deepened. "What would Blondie say?"

He blinked. "Who?"

"Your girlfriend."

It took him a moment. "Oh, Stacy. She'd probably be texting or tweeting or something and never notice the scenery."

"I wasn't talking about the scenery."

"No?"

"What would she say about the way you are staring at me?"

"I'm not staring at you. I was studying the instrument panel," he lied smoothly, his stomach roiling and unsettled.

"Uh-huh."

Well, damn, if she didn't want men to look at her, she shouldn't wear shorts like that. "You do have nice legs."

"So does Blondie."

He blew out his breath. "I think you must have gotten the wrong idea about Stacy and I."

"I think I understand it pretty well."

"We're just…" What were they?

Sophia turned toward him, arched an eyebrow. "Friends with benefits?"

The benefit part was right, the friend part, not so much. "Could we talk about something else?"

"It is your three thousand dollars. We can talk about whatever you want."

Silence stretched out wide as the sky. He had to fix that. He should ask Sophia something else. "How long have you been a pilot?"

"I got my pilot's license when I was sixteen," she said proudly.

"Wow, that's young."

"My father's a pilot. This was his plane. He gave it to me when he retired."

"Why did he retire?"

"He's losing his sight."

"That's a shame."

Sophia nodded. "Yes. Poppy is like a bird with a broken wing. It's very sad."

"You speak English like a native," he said. "Much better than my Spanish."

"I was bilingual even as a kid. I have dual citizenship. My mother was an American," she said. "We visited her family in California every Christmas."

"Where abouts in California?"

"Ventura."

"Really? I have a beach house in Santa Barbara."

"Of course you do," she said.

"What's that tone all about?"

"What tone?"

"The tone that says there's something wrong with having a lot of money."

She gave a half laugh that sounded more like a snort. "You are imagining things, Mr. Martin. I do not have a tone."

Was he? "You don't have anything against wealthy people?"

"Why would I have such an attitude? If it were not for the rich and powerful and famous who come to Bosque de Los Dioses, I would not have a job."

"Because I know how some rich people can be. They can be very demanding. I'm sure you have to put up with a lot."

A sly smile flitted across her face. "Ah."

"Ah, what?"

She shook her head.

"What is it?"

"You are the one with the prejudice against the wealthy."

"What! That's crazy. I'm worth over a billion dollars." Well, until this last investment, but he would be back up there again soon. "Why would I be prejudice against rich people? That's like saying I'm prejudiced against myself."

"Are you?"

"Am I what?"

"Prejudiced against yourself?"

What kind of question was that? He shifted uncomfortably in his seat. "No."

"You weren't born into money," she said.

How had she guessed? He raised his chin. "What makes you assume that?"

"That chip sitting on your shoulder."

"I don't have a chip—" Shut up. Don't argue with her. It doesn't matter.

"Were you?" she asked. "Born rich?"

"No," he admitted.

"So you are a self-made man."

"There's that tone again. You're mocking me."

"You are mistaking my jovial nature for mocking."

"Am I?" Gibb shook his head. The woman was turning him inside out and he couldn't say why. Sure she was cute and sexy, but so were a million other women. What was it about this one that stoked him and frustrated him and challenged him and made him want to grab her up and kiss her until neither one of them could breathe?

"This is going to be a very long flight, isn't it?"

"It sure is shaping up that way."

More silence. This time he wasn't going to say anything. He could sit here forever and be quiet if need be. Not a word. Not another word was going to pass his lips.

She looked out over the nose of the plane, and with the slightest moments, shifted the plane northward. Underneath her breath she was softly humming, "Don't Worry, Be Happy."

"Okay," he blurted. "You're right. Maybe I do have a chip on my shoulder."

"I know."

Did she have to sound so damn cheerful about it? Gibb clamped his teeth together. Not another word.

"About that chip on your shoulder?" she ventured.

"Yes?"

"It's due to a sense of inadequacy."

"Inadequacy? Where are you getting this stuff?"

"Why else would you resent what you are?"

"I don't resent who I am."

"Don't you?"

"Thank you, oh, doctor of psychology." He wiped his brow. "Okay, I'll bite."

"Bite what?"

"The bait."

"What bait?"

While she might speak English like a native, the idioms seemed to throw her. "You throw out a challenging line like it's the bait. So here I am, biting it like a fish."

"Um, all right."

"What do you mean by the chip on my shoulder is due to a sense of inadequacy?"

Sophia shrugged. She was totally nonchalant. How did one get to be so blasé about everything? "You feel like you don't deserve your riches."

Gibb coughed, tugged at his collar. He felt like she'd

taken an endoscope and shoved it down his throat and could see everything that was happening inside his gut. Exposed. He felt totally exposed and he didn't like it, not in the least.

She glanced at him. "Are you all right?"

"Fine," he said tightly and coughed again.

"Sometimes the high altitude—"

"It's not the altitude."

"Maybe if you took off your tie."

"I'm fine."

Momentarily, she held up both palms, before her beautiful hands settled back down on the yoke. That smile of hers could seriously blind a guy. It was unnatural to be that happy.

Gibb took off his tie, undid the top button of his dress shirt. Instantly, he could breathe better.

She laid an index finger over her lips. "Shh, I promise that I won't tell anyone if you take off the jacket, too."

"I'm good."

"As you wish."

A long silence began as they passed over blue water and a lot of land. He hadn't been this knocked off balance since the last time a corporate spy ripped him off.

She was back to humming, "Don't Worry, Be Happy." It ought to be illegal for anyone to be this cheerful.

He stared out the side window, studied lush green ground sliding by. How many times had he flown over a place like this, oblivious to the lives of the people below? "How did you know?"

She startled as if she had forgotten that he was in the plane with her. "Know what?"

"That I wasn't born wealthy."

She clicked her tongue. "You work so hard. Too hard."

"Rich people work hard."

"Old money knows how to relax, new money scrambles. You scramble like you're afraid someone will take it all away."

"Now you sound like a fortune cookie."

She seemed to take no offense at that. "Maybe. And you spend money heedlessly. I saw you give Stacy that limitless black credit card. She is at the spa every day splurging on treatments with your money. People who are born rich tend to be frugal."

"That's a generalization."

"True."

"So what if I work hard and spend easily?" Stop being defensive. You don't owe her an explanation. "I still don't see how you drew your conclusion."

"In two weeks time you never took off the suits."

He ran a hand over the sleeve of his silk Armani.

"Not once."

"I took them off to go to bed."

"But not when people could see you. I had to ask myself why. Why does this handsome, successful man drive himself so hard? He's supposed to be on vacation and he never takes off the suit. What is he so afraid of?" She paused. "And then it hit me."

"What did?"

"You never felt loved for who you were."

Goose bumps spread over his arms at the same time the hairs on the nape of his neck lifted. He tried to laugh, but he just exhaled harshly.

"So you drove yourself hard in order to get recognition. Status became everything."

His throat worked, but no words came out.

"You became adept at charming others. You adopted whatever image worked. It's why you wear expensive suits—status, attention getting, uniform of the wealthy."

Gibb's mouth dropped open. How did she know!

"You came to feel that it was not okay to be who you really were, that in order to be loved, you had to take on the feelings and identity of those whose love you wished to win."

He wanted to deny it. He felt the need to contradict her, but he was so floored that he simply couldn't find the words.

"Deep down inside," she went on, "you believe that no matter how much success you achieve you'll always be a failure. You feel like a fraud."

He planned to say, "Hell, no, you're crazy, you're nuts," but instead Gibb simply nodded and said, "Empty."

"This friend of yours that you're flying to see. The one you want to stop from getting married. He's known you a long time?"

"Yeah." Gibb grunted.

"Before you were rich."

"Uh-huh."

"He's the only one who knows who you really are, isn't he?"

Was the woman some kind of psychic or just perceptive as hell? "How…how can you possibly know this?"

She met his gaze. "Why, it's written all over you. Anyone who bothers to look past the suit can see it."

4

BESIDES FLYING, Sophia's one great talent was the ability to read people quickly. She couldn't explain her skill. It was intuitive. Perhaps it came from being the youngest of seven, where in order to get her way, she had to figure out what everyone else's angle was and use it to her advantage. Or maybe it was simply because she loved people, and found them fascinating.

Unfortunately, she'd learned the hard way that most people did not enjoy being sized up. Usually, she kept her opinions to herself, but something about Gibb had loosened her tongue.

Now he sat there scowling at her as if she'd given him a bad tarot card reading. For many hours it would be just him and her together in this tiny cockpit.

"You should be proud that you are a self-made man," she said, trying to smooth things over.

"But you see, I'm not."

"If you weren't born rich and you're not a self-made man, then where did you get your money from?" she asked.

"My mother married a rich man. He adopted me."

"And he died and left you all this money?"

"No, James is still very much alive."

"He simply gave you a billion dollars?"

"Of course not. I earned my own money."

"Then you are a self-made man."

Gibb shook his head. "I couldn't have done it without James's connections."

"So you are in the same business he's in?"

"No. He's in real estate, I made my first few million creating a game app for phones when that industry was just taking off."

"Like Angry Birds?"

"Something along those lines."

"What is the app called?"

"Zimdiggy."

"Oh! I've played that game. It's fun. I love all the detailed levels. Have you invented more game apps?"

"I sold out to a big gaming company, then I became a venture capitalist. I'm not really an idea guy."

"What does that mean?"

"I'm more of a moneyman, backing other people's inventions. I seem to have a knack for predicting the next big thing and I'm not afraid to take risks."

It was odd, this self-effacing side of him. It didn't match with his confident outer persona.

"Really? You'd rather work yourself into the ground just to keep getting richer than do something fun that you love?"

"It's not about getting richer. It's about seeing how much I can achieve."

"So achievement is your passion, not creating your own game apps?"

"This way, I help other people achieve their dreams."

"Your game app helps people. I can't tell you how much Zimdiggy kept my mind distracted while I sat at my father's hospital bed after his eye surgery."

A brief smile flitted over his lips.

"When do *you* get to enjoy the fruits of your labor?" she asked.

"My labor is the fruit," he said it as if he really believed it, but a faraway expression in his eyes belied the words.

Poor guy. He was unhappy and didn't even know it, but she wasn't about to point that out. He'd just deny it anyway. "So see, you *are* self-made."

"I wouldn't have made it without my adopted father's help."

"What's wrong with that?"

"I feel like I'm only where I'm at by a twist of fate. If James had married someone other than my mother, some other guy would be here instead of me."

"You underestimate yourself, Mr. Martin."

"Gibb," he said. "Call me Gibb, we've got a long flight ahead of us and when you call me Mr. Martin, I think of my stepfather."

"Even though he adopted you, you still don't think of him as your father?"

"He's a tough man to get to know. I don't want to sound ungrateful because he's done a lot for me and my mother, but he and I never really bonded, you know?"

Sophia didn't know. Her father was her best friend. "So you are an only child."

"Yes."

"What happened to your real father?"

"Who knows? Dead maybe, or in prison? He left my mom when I was a baby. I never knew him."

"You have no desire to seek him out?"

"None at all."

How sad. She cast a sideways glance over at him. The man was a tight ball of barely contained energy, his hands curled into fists against his upper thighs. She remembered how he'd paced the balcony of his bungalow, restless as a tiger. He was not a man who sat still easily.

A sweet shiver, like fingers gliding over piano keys, ran up and down her spine.

Beneath the kumquat and leather notes of his cologne, she caught the scent of something deeper, more primal and masculine. Raw, sexual heat from his body radiated across the confined space, and crashed headlong into her.

Did he feel it, too? Or was it all in her imagination?

His gaze flicked to her legs again and something in his eyes flared hot. Oh, yes. He was feeling it, too.

When was the last time she'd felt such a strong instant attraction to anyone? His gaze tracked from her legs to her breasts with an expression so sultry she could hardly breathe. Um, never?

Who was she kidding? A man like Gibb Martin could never be interested in her. Not for the long haul at any rate.

She wouldn't need him for the long haul. One hot night in his arms would do the trick.

Mmm. It was a delicious but dangerous thought.

Just thinking about having sex with him had her going soft and pliant in all the right places.

That light gray silk suit had clearly been tailored to fit his body. His hair was as sandy as the beaches of Limon, and cut short and neat.

She lowered her eyelids, looked at him through the

fringe of her lashes, hoping he would think that she was inspecting the instrument panel and not him.

Be honest, Sophia.

No point lying to herself. She was flat out ogling him. Who wouldn't ogle? The man had splendid bone structure and firm, elegant muscles—hard, but not bulky.

He was magnificent.

Gulping, she shifted her attention back to the landscape. They had passed over the center of Costa Rica, which, at its widest point, was only one hundred and eight miles across, and were headed toward the Caribbean Sea. Before long, they would be entering Nicaraguan air space.

"Sophia," Gibb murmured.

Had he said her name or had she imagined it. Between the sound of the engine and the headset, she had trouble hearing him.

She turned her head again to find him staring at her. "Yes?"

"Are you married?"

The question took her by surprise, so did the heated flush that raced to her cheeks. She held up her left hand so he could see it was bare of a ring.

"Boyfriend?"

Good question. She still hadn't told Emilio that they would not be taking their relationship to the next level. He was such a nice guy, but it wasn't fair of her to string him along when she did not have any romantic feelings for him.

She studied the instrument panel, the tachometer reading, the fuel system cluster, the altimeter and temperature gauges. Everything was fine.

"Sophia?"

"Emilio is not my boyfriend any more so than Stacy is your girlfriend," she finally answered.

"Ah," he said. "A friend with benefits."

She owed him no explanation about her relationship status. She would let him think whatever he wanted.

"So no one serious?"

Why was he asking? She lifted a shoulder. "I'm too young to get serious."

"How old are you?"

"Did anyone ever tell you that it's not polite to ask a woman her age." She maneuvered the plane through puffs of late-afternoon cloud.

"I'm thirty-two," he volunteered.

He was older than she would have guessed. "Twenty-six," she admitted.

"And you're still not ready to settle down?"

"Are you?"

He chuckled. "No, no, I'm not."

That killed the conversation.

Good. She needed to concentrate on what she was doing. They were about to cross over into Nicaragua. She radioed the nearest air tower with her intentions and was cleared. They were cruising along at seven thousand feet and a hundred and thirty knots per hour.

But soon, the silence got to her, which was odd. Normally, she was happy as a clam when she was in the air and nothing upset her equilibrium. She canted her head, studied him from the corner of her eye.

He was handsome enough to be a movie star, especially when he flashed that grin. He was such an enigma. On the one hand, a serious workaholic, underneath though, there was a playful side he'd buried long ago to please a stepfather who, from Gibb's account, withheld affection while at the same time, freely gave him material things. Such mixed messages must be very confusing.

"May I ask you a personal question?" she asked.

"Nothing has stopped you so far," he said.

"You do not have to answer if you don't want to."

"Let's hear it. What's on your mind?"

"What is it that you want most in life, Mr. Martin?"

"Gibb," he said. "You can call me Gibb. Maybe you should tell me what I want, Sophia, since you just did such a good job of reading me."

"Ah, but if I do it for you then you don't have to do any soul searching."

"Soul searching is overrated. I'm more goal oriented than emotive."

"You're avoiding the question."

"You said I didn't have to answer."

"I've changed my mind. Emote."

"Anyone ever tell you that you can be a bit bossy?"

"In other words, you have no idea what it is that you want from life?"

"I want for nothing. I'm living the dream."

"And yet, you do not seem happy."

For a long time he said nothing. "What do you mean?"

"Never mind. I don't know you. I shouldn't have said anything."

"No, really. Go on. I want to hear your thoughts."

"It's just that…"

"What?"

"When will you have enough money to earn your stepfather's love?"

"That's not what I'm doing."

"All right."

"It's not."

"You never did answer my question about what it is you want."

"Food. I'm starving. I forgot to eat lunch. You got anything to eat?" he asked.

She didn't poke his answer. She'd done enough prodding. "There are snacks in a box in the seat behind you."

He undid his seat belt; twisted around, found the box of snacks. "Hey, graham crackers. I haven't had those since I was a kid."

"They're my favorite."

"You ever make s'mores?"

"I've got the makings for s'mores in that box."

"And so you do!" he said, pulling out a bag of marshmallows and some chocolate bars. "How come you fly around with the makings for s'mores in your plane?"

"I take my nieces and nephews out camping sometimes."

He crunched a graham cracker, held one out to her.

She took the cracker and their fingers brushed in the handoff. His touch ignited something hot and irresistible inside her. To distract herself, she stuck the cracker in her mouth.

"I haven't made s'mores since Scott and I camped out in his parents' backyard, like I said," Gibb mused.

Sophia tried to imagine him as a young boy, but she couldn't picture it. "Maybe you two could make s'mores again. Once you break up his wedding."

"You're making me sound like an ass."

"I never said that."

"You didn't have to."

"Sounds to me like you're feeling guilty," she commented.

"About how long do you think it will take for us to get to Key West?" he asked.

"Factoring in fuel stops, depending on the weather, I'd say at least fifteen hours. Maybe fourteen, if we're lucky and don't run into a headwind, but it could be longer."

"Is this as fast as the plane will go?"

"Yes. If you wanted faster, you should have called for a private jet."

"Privacy is more important than speed at this point," he said.

"Then sit back and relax and let me do my job."

"I'm not very good at that."

"What? Letting go of control or relaxing?"

"Either. Both."

"All the more reason to surrender," she said.

"Easy to say, not so easy to do."

"Close your eyes and take a deep breath."

"I'd—"

"I'm the pilot," she interrupted. "It's an order."

"Are you always this bossy?"

"Only with certain clients."

He surprised her by closing his eyes and taking deep breaths.

Sometime later, she peeked over at him again. Gibb was sound asleep. Good.

They had passed over Nicaragua and were above the Caribbean Sea. She peered out the window and through the wisp of clouds, spied a petite lush green jungle island with a thin apron of beach lying due south. The island looked completely uninhabited, no roads, no structures, too small and isolated for anyone to live there. It wasn't even on the aerial map. What a thrill. Discovering a place she'd never known existed.

For the next several minutes, she navigated smoothly through patches of harmless midlevel, horizontal altostratus clouds with a flat, uniform structure. The fine mist of the altostratus parted easily and caused no turbulence.

She had radioed the last tower before leaving Nicaraguan airspace. She'd wanted an update on the tropical storm brewing in the Caribbean and received an all clear about the weather. So it was something of a surprise when she sailed through the last batch of stratus clouds and came face-to-face with a wide, vertical band of wooly clouds. They were in the exact direction where they needed to fly.

Sophia sighed. "Shoot."

Gibb opened one eye. "What is it?"

"Cumulus."

"Cum what?" He straightened in the seat, opened his other eye and instantly wore a cocky expression on his handsome face.

She ignored his innuendo, ignored the spark of sexual awareness zipping through her. "Cumulus clouds. Although at this elevation they're called alto cumulus. A small street of them might be just bumpy, but they can be dangerous for small planes to fly through because they are formed in unstable air that is always trying to rise higher."

"So there is a chance for updrafts."

"Yes, and if the cumulus clouds gain moisture at higher altitudes, they turn into cumulonimbus clouds."

"Sounds like sex on a bus," he teased.

"It's not funny," she said. As happy-go-lucky and adventuresome as Sophia might be, when it came to flying, she did not make jokes or take weather lightly.

"What does this mean?"

"It means I'm not laughing about the cumulus clouds."

"Not that," he said. "Can we fly through them?"

"We could, but it could be much more than just a bumpy ride. Look how wide and thick they are. I wouldn't know the extent of how far they ranged until we were in the middle of them. And it might take as long as an hour to do it and I simply can't risk that."

"Don't you have some kind of radar or sonar or something to tell you this stuff?"

"Who do you think I am? The weatherman? You see anything on this 1971 control panel that looks like it could track a storm?"

"No."

"This plane isn't built for long-haul flying. I tried to tell you that."

"So what do we do?"

"We fly around the clouds."

"How long will that take?"

"It's weather. I don't have a crystal ball."

"Can you call a tower and ask?"

"There are no manned towers out here. I could call UNICOM, but they'd just tell me to fly around it."

Gibb drummed his fingers against the door. "Dammit."

"You said earlier that privacy is more important than speed. I'll get you there in plenty of time to break up your friend's wedding, even with the delay."

"I thought the tropical storm was two days away."

"This isn't part of the storm. If it were, the air traffic controllers in Nicaragua would have advised me to land. We're okay on that score."

Gibb chuffed out his breath, stabbed his fingers through his hair.

"You don't take detours in stride, do you?" she asked.

"Why should I?"

"Can't control Mother Nature."

The cumulus clouds were getting closer, stretching out across the corridor of their immediate path. The only part of the sky clear of cumulus clouds was due south. The opposite direction of where they needed to go.

Having little alternative, Sophia headed south. She wouldn't admit it to Gibb, but she was nervous. She'd never flown over the Caribbean and the army of cumulus clouds was not making life any easier. Still, there was no reason for any real alarm.

Everything was looking good, until she directed the plane eastward, hoping to skirt the cumulus clouds, and got caught up in a ferocious headwind. It pushed back against El Diablo with a speed of more than a hundred and sixty knots per hour.

Sophia battled against the wind, trying to hold the plane steady. The nose kept dipping and she struggled to keep it up. They rolled like a body surfer trying to navigate the waves off Oahu's North Shore. Her hands tensed on the yoke, tightening muscles all the way up to her shoulders.

"What's going on?" Gibb demanded.

"Hush!" Sophia snapped.

To her surprise, he did.

She took the plane lower, hoping the maneuver would

lessen the push of the headwind, dropping down to four thousand feet. The Caribbean sparkled impossibly blue below them.

They were making no headway. Salmon swimming upstream had a better chance of getting where they were going. Initially, she'd hoped the headwind would slack off, but it only seemed to grow stronger. Her gaze focused on the gas gauge, less than half a tank remaining.

"We have to go back," she told Gibb.

"Why?"

"We're running low on fuel."

"We're running out of gas? I thought you fueled up before we left."

"We did, but a headwind this strong pulls fuel from the tank like water running out of a flushing toilet. If I don't make a decision right now, we won't have enough gas to make it back to Nicaragua."

"Is there somewhere closer we could land, fuel up and wait for the weather conditions to improve?"

Or even put him on a commercial liner. Truth be told, she was ready to get rid of Gibb Martin and get back to her nice, simple life of ferrying tourists back and forth from Libera to Bosque de Los Dioses.

"Well?"

She blew out her breath. "There's Island de Providencia."

"Let's go there."

"One problem."

"What's that?"

"The island lies due north. We'd have to fly right through the cumulus clouds to get there."

"Do we have enough gas to make it?"

"Theoretically, but there's no guarantee. Not with the

strength of these headwinds. Not in this plane where I cannot fly above the cumulus clouds."

"So returning to Nicaragua is our best option?"

"Yes."

He swore under his breath.

"What is the big deal? Is stopping your friend's wedding worth risking our lives over?"

"I just wish there was an alternative to returning to Nicaragua."

"Well, there's not." Sophia turned the plane back in a southerly direction. Once they were headed west, the headwind would become a tailwind, and at that point, an advantage.

That's when the engine sputtered.

It was probably just an air bubble in the fuel line, nothing to worry about. She kept turning El Diablo, but to be on the safe side, she went down another thousand feet.

"What was that?" Gibb asked.

"Just a stutter in the engine," she reassured him.

"It doesn't sound good."

"It's an old plane. These things happen sometimes."

Gibb looked skeptical. "You're worried about it, too. That's why you've dropped altitude."

"No reason to be alarmed. It's always better to be safe than sorry," she said. Okay, she could handle this. She'd been trained by the best—her father.

"Yes, but your plane should at least be airworthy."

She glared at him. "My plane is plenty airworthy."

The engine sputtered again.

"Oh, yeah?"

"Most likely it's a cylinder misfiring from running the fuel mixture too rich," she said, ignoring the prickle of anxiety crawling through her stomach. She kept El Diablo in peak condition, but still… "Easy fix. I'll just lean up the mixture."

"What does that mean?"

"Leaning it up adds air to the fuel ratio." She pulled back on the orange handled fuel rod, while at the same time, keeping her eye on the tachometer, until the needle hit the optimal revolutions per minute on the gauge.

"Why didn't you already lean it up?"

"Because you want richer fuel at a higher altitude." She paused, listened to the engine, and heard nothing. Felt nothing. Good. That seemed to have fixed it.

She settled back into the seat. They were headed due west now. The tension eased from her shoulders. Sophia was about to reach for the radio to call into the nearest tower, when the engine sputtered again, this time louder and longer.

"So much for the fuel mixture theory," Gibb said.

Alarmed, but determined not to show it, she ran through her head all the possible causes for the engine cutting out. Maybe it was bad spark plugs? But she'd just changed them out a couple of weeks ago. Maybe she hadn't tightened down a wire?

She dropped down another five hundred feet.

"You take this puppy any lower and I'm going to need to put on my swim trunks."

If she hadn't had all her attention on the plane, she might have teased him and told him she didn't know he owned a pair of swim trunks. Or had an erotic fantasy about how sexy he would look bare-chested and dressed for a swim. As it was, she clenched her teeth tight and remembered everything she'd learned about how to make an emergency landing. It was something every pilot was taught, but hoped never to use.

The engine sputtered a forth time.

Her heart pounded. *Don't panic, don't panic.* "Gotta get this plane on the ground and take a look at that engine," she muttered to herself.

"What?" Gibb sat up straighter. "Where?"

"There." She pointed at the small, uninhabited island they'd flown over earlier.

"What's that?"

"An island."

"The size of a breath mint."

The engine sputtered, shuddered. "You got any better ideas?" she asked.

"You mean besides a crash landing?"

"An emergency landing," she corrected. "I'm going to do my best not to crash."

"We're going to crash!"

"There's a small strip of beach," she persisted as they flew closer. However, at this lower altitude she could see the spot was not nearly as big as she'd first thought and what there was of it was littered with driftwood and coconuts.

Not ideal at all, but it was their only option.

The engine sputtered again, cut out. Had to be the stupid carburetor. What could be wrong with the carburetor?

"Hang on," she yelled. "We're going down."

5

THE BELLY OF the plane skimmed the tops of the thick jungle forest. Fronds and branches slapped and scraped against metal producing a loud screeching noise. Gibb cringed, and grabbed on to his seat with both hands to brace himself for the fall and speared a glance at Sophia.

Sweat beaded her brow, her top teeth were sunk deep into her bottom lip, but her eyes were narrowed in grim determination and her expression declared, *Come hell or high water, I'm landing this plane on this island.*

That is, unless they overshot it.

Which, considering the compact size of the island and the thinness of the beach, seemed more likely with every passing second.

Damn those spies who'd freaked him out so much he'd chartered a plane that had no business doing anything more than ferrying tourists from airports to mountaintop resorts. Damn Scott for being so irrational and marrying a woman he'd only known for a month.

Hey, while you're at it, why not damn yourself? You're the one who allowed emotion to overrule common sense and you're the one who told her to keep flying instead of turning back like she wanted to.

Yes, okay, damn his hide for that.

Honestly, he was amazed at her calm skill. He knew grown men who would be whimpering like little girls in a similar situation. Hell, a yelp or two might have jumped out of his throat.

But Sophia was in complete control. Well, as much as anyone could be in control during a forced landing. Nervous as he was, he still had the utmost confidence in her ability to land this thing without killing them.

Unsecured items bounced around the cockpit. The box of snacks flew open, raining cookies, crackers, candy bars, marshmallows and bags of chips all around them. Stuff in the back of the plane shifted, slid, skidded.

With all the flying he'd done in his life, he'd grown lackadaisical. Taken it for granted that any plane he was on would stay airborne. Statistics bore him out. The chances of being killed in a plane crash were miniscule, but planes did go down. Small, old planes more so than others.

Hubris. He was full of hubris thinking he was immune. When had this sense of entitlement overtaken him? That he was somehow too special for any plane he was flying in to experience a mishap? He hadn't been born that way. In fact, when he was a kid, he'd felt anything but special. Maybe that was the reason why he'd worked so hard to be rich—the need to be special.

Where had that flash of insight come from? He wasn't particularly self-aware. He had, in fact, on more than one occasion, been accused of being oblivious in regard to his inner motivations. C'mon, who sat around and thought about stuff like that?

Apparently, during an emergency landing, he did.

The wheels touched down hard.

Gibb's head snapped back, his teeth clacked together. Had they hit the ground or something else? Hell, he had his eyes squeezed closed and every muscle in his body was coiled tight as new box springs.

The plane jolted, shuddered, stopped.

"We're okay," Sophia said.

Gibb wiped his sweaty palms over his knees and pried his eyes open.

The plane was tilting to the left. The late-afternoon sun shining through the windshield illuminated drifting dust motes on a shaft of light. Everything was eerily silent.

Then the back end of the plane dropped a few inches.

They both jumped. Laughed nervously.

"Best crash landing I've ever had," he said.

"How many crash landings have you had?"

"First one."

"So you're really experienced."

He shouldn't be smiling in this situation, or teasing, but he couldn't help it. "Seen it all."

"Aren't I lucky to be with the most experienced passenger in the world."

Hey, she was teasing back. Why not? "How about you?" he asked. "How many times have you crash landed?"

Her cute little chin hardened. "I'm not in the habit of crashing planes if that's what you're suggesting."

Oops, he'd gone too far. He raised both palms and

surrendered. "I wasn't taking potshots at your flying abilities."

"It sounded like you were."

"Now your mechanic's abilities…" He shrugged, gave her a deadpan expression. "Maybe."

She looked as if she'd just bitten into a lemon when she was expecting an orange. "I'm my own mechanic."

Great. Open mouth insert foot yet again. "Joke. I was joking."

"I overhauled the engine this year in mechanic school. With the teacher's supervision, I might add."

"You just finished mechanic school?" Ouch. He had to stop stepping on her toes.

"I'm a good mechanic," she bristled. "Top in my class."

"I'm sure you were."

"I was the only woman in the class."

Anything he said at this point was bound to backfire. Go with an honest compliment. "Really, that landing was amazing."

"You're just trying to placate me."

He was. "Look, I have a tendency to spout stuff off the top of my head. Ignore me."

"I did a thorough flight check before we took off and two weeks ago I did routine maintenance, changed the oil and spark plugs. Sometimes things just happen in spite of excellent maintenance."

"You're feeling guilty. Don't feel guilty. I was joking. You're easygoing. I thought you would get the joke."

"Easygoing about life, not about my plane."

"Duly noted. No more plane jokes."

"But what if it's my fault?" she fretted. "What if I didn't tighten a loose wire or—"

"Listen, if it was your fault, then you can feel guilty, but even if the malfunction was somehow your fault, you did land us safely. You get props for that." This was odd. He was the customer. He should be the one obsessing about the crash, not trying to make her feel better. But the poor woman looked so woebegone.

"I should have known ahead of time about that stack of cumulus clouds. I should have—"

"Spilled milk," he said. "Let it go. No point wringing your hands over something that's already happened. Let's just get a towel and mop up that milk."

Problem solver. That was his M.O. If you could fix a problem, then just fix it. If not, figure out how to move on. No point wallowing in recrimination or pointing fingers. Deal with the situation as it was. The plan had worked for him so far.

"I'm so sorry."

Gibb unbuckled his seat belt. "Don't apologize. Find out what happened to the plane and repair it so we can be on our way again."

"That sounds good," she said. "And of course I will try to do that, but it might not be as easy as it sounds. Complications have a way of arising."

"We find a complication, we'll deal with it."

She unbuckled her own seat belt, looked around at the debris littering the cockpit and sighed deeply. "Like the majority of North Americans, you're extremely goal oriented. If there is a ball, you must kick it. If there is food, you must eat it. If there is a mountain you must climb it."

"Costa Ricans don't care about goals?" Actually, this was part of the problem he'd encountered while trying to get things done in Costa Rica. People moved at a snail's pace compared to life in the U.S.

"*Ticos* are generally more interested in relationships than outcomes," she said. "We would rather enjoy our family and friends than rush around chasing some meaningless goal," she said.

"Meaningless? You call making money meaningless?"

"Do you have more than you can spend?"

"More money than I could spend in ten lifetimes."

"Then why does making more money matter?"

The question stopped him cold. He had no answer. "I'm going to Key West because of a relationship," he said. "If my purpose was a goal, I would let my friend make a big mistake and I'd stay focused on my project."

"Instead you are in neither place. I am sorry, Mr. Martin."

"Stop apologizing. I'm cool with the fact we had to crash land. Things happen. I get that. Let's just get a move on and get things repaired so we can fly out of here ASAP."

She looked dubious. "It would be a good idea to manage your expectations. I will try my best, but there might not be a quick fix."

"You said you were part American, now's the time to draw on that Yankee ingenuity and kick the lamentations to the curb." He pounded his fist into his palm in a gesture he used to get his employees fired up.

"This is why people find some Americans off-putting. They tend to think that their way is always the best way."

He straightened the lapels of his jacket. So what if he thought his way was the best way? Didn't everyone?

You did what worked for you. That's why it was your way. "I put you off?"

"I didn't say me. I was simply pointing out cultural differences. I get to do that since I have roots in both cultures."

"I understand your point, but can we save the cultural sensitivity discussion for later? I'm kind of in a hurry here."

She shook her head and he could have sworn she mumbled, "Impossible."

He decided to let it go, pulled the latch on the door, and tried to shove it open. It moved, but no more than an inch before it hit something and wouldn't budge any farther. "What the...?"

"One of those expectations that requires management," she said lightly.

He huffed. Okay, he was in another country. There was always some culture shock involved. He could handle it. Just as long as she got this heap running in time to get him on his way to Florida to stop Scott's 4:00 p.m. wedding on Saturday.

Sophia tried her door and it opened with ease. She crooked a finger at him. "This way."

He climbed out, following her.

She stood on the beach at the front of the plane, surveying their situation, her delicate hands resting on her curvy hips.

He imagined her in a red string bikini and his heart rate kicked up a notch. Down, boy. Not the time, nor the place. Think of something else.

The plane wasn't level. The tire on the pilot's side of the plane was sunk into the sand. The other tire was parked on a large fallen tree. Jungle vines were whipped around the door handle. That's what had prevented him from getting out. But other than the imbalanced landing position, the plane didn't look too bad.

"What now?" he asked.

"I have to find out what made the engine sputter. If it's something repairable, I'll repair it. Then we have to figure out how to get the plane on even ground so that we can take off from the beach."

He glanced over his shoulder. The sea was only a couple of yards behind them. There certainly didn't seem to be enough of a makeshift runway to achieve liftoff, not that he knew much about it. He had to find another way off this island as quickly as he could. No offense against Sophia Cruz's mechanical skills or her flying abilities, but Gibb felt insecure without a backup plan.

"I'll get my tools," she said and crawled back inside the plane.

Gibb pulled his cell phone from his pocket and walked a short distance away. To the left of the plane lay a thicket of jungle trees, much like those found in the rain forest of Costa Rica. The island might not be big, probably no more than five miles long and three miles across, but it was high. Rocky outcroppings in the middle of the island jutted a good thousand feet into the air. He tried the phone.

No service.

Well, what did you expect way out here in the middle of nowhere? Certainly not cell phone reception. Grunting, he pocketed the device.

Sophia emerged from the plane with a red canvas tool bag. She had her pink cowboy hat fixed firmly on her head. "You're not going to get cell phone reception."

"So I figured. Show me how to use the radio. I want to call for help."

"We're probably out of range from an air tower," she said. "And besides, by the time we could get someone out here, I could have the plane repaired."

"In time to take off tonight?" He eyed the sun dipping toward the horizon.

"Probably not," she said. "I'm not taking off in the dark. Not from here."

"What if it's not an easy fix?"

"Let us cross that bridge when we come to it."

"Humor me. Let me try the radio."

"If you insist, but even if you did manage to raise someone on the radio, they're not going to helicopter Navy SEALs in here to rescue you. They'll send a boat, but not until daylight. We'll be here for the night, so chill."

"I don't do that very well," Gibb growled.

"Then make yourself useful."

"How's that?"

Her critical gaze skated over him, as she took in his suit. Fine. It wasn't beachwear, but he hadn't known he was going to end up on the beach.

"You could help me, hand me tools as I need them, or…"

He didn't much like the sound of that. Too passive. "Or what?"

"Go gather some driftwood and make a fire."

He stared at her. "A fire?"

"You do know how to make a fire, don't you?" She made rubbing motions as if she were using kindling. "Just rub two sticks together and glow."

Gibb grinned. "Nice riff on Lauren Bacall's character in *Key Largo*."

"To Have and Have Not."

"To have what?"

"The movie. The line isn't from *Key Largo*. It's from *To Have and Have Not*."

"No kidding?"

"I wouldn't lie to you."

"Maybe. I don't really know you."

She drew herself up to her full five foot two. "I am not a liar, Mr. Martin."

He was putting her off again. "I'll take your word for it. From now on I'll assume you're telling the truth. How do you know so much about old movies?"

"My mother was a movie buff. Sometimes when I'm feeling sentimental, I watch the classics."

"I wouldn't have suspected you had a sentimental bone in your body, Amelia."

"Why? Because I'm a pilot?"

"Because you're so grounded."

She laughed. "You missed the part about me being a pilot?"

"I'm not talking about your profession, but rather your personality."

"Thanks. I think." She turned and walked away.

He hadn't made a campfire in so long. When, and if, he ever found himself in need of a fire, he paid someone to make it for him. "What do we need a fire for?"

She stopped and looked at him over the shoulder as if he were the dumbest creature to ever roam the earth. "Light. Heat. Keep the mosquitoes away. To cook dinner."

"Dinner? Where are we going to get food? Beyond those junk food snacks in the plane."

She gave him a Mona Lisa smile. "If you're going to start the fire, I suggest you collect driftwood before it gets too dark to see where you're walking."

"I can gather all the driftwood in the world, but how am I supposed to light it without a match or lighter?"

"If you ask nicely, I'll let you use the matches in my emergency kit." She gave him a dazzling smile.

The smile did something to him. Lit him up inside in a way that left him feeling decidedly unsettled. "I'll just get at it, then."

"You do that," she said. "Now that you have a goal, I'm sure you feel better."

Dazzled and dazed, Gibb left her to gather wood. He was out of sorts from the crash landing, that's all this attraction was, nothing more. Yeah, okay, she was gorgeous and her legs in those skimpy cutoffs made him feel as if he'd just swallowed his own tongue, but it was nothing more than lust with an element of added danger.

With any luck, they'd be on their way by morning. As long as he kept his hands to himself, he ought to be fine.

Gibb swiveled around for another look.

Sophia was bent over, examining the plane's fixed landing gear, her delectable little fanny in the air. The pockets of her cutoff jeans stretched tight.

His tongue was notably plastered to the roof of his mouth and he instantly grew as stiff as an ironing board. Ignoring the sand filling his dress shoes, he turned and started picking up driftwood before he did something drastic that he could not undo.

Like seduce her.

SOPHIA TOED HER sneakers off—her mind worked better when her feet were bare—and set about inspecting the plane. Her toes sank into the sand, anchoring her to the earth. Grounded. A reminder to focus on what she was doing and keep her mind off how absurdly sexy Gibb looked standing on the beach in his fancy clothes. She half expected a men's fashion photographer to pop up and start snapping pictures of him.

Here was the thing. Gibb aroused her in a way no man ever had. That passion she'd told Josie about. Every time Gibb's hot-eyed gaze landed on her, she felt as if she would burst into flames.

Simmer down. She didn't have to act on her feelings. Except she and Gibb were stuck on an isolated island in the Caribbean Sea with nothing to do but either fix the plane or wait to be rescued. As of yet, she didn't know what was wrong with El Diablo.

Maybe she could repair it, maybe not.

She had taken off without doing anything more than filing a flight plan. They were out of radio contact range from any air tower. Her family had no idea where she was and when she'd gone to make those phone calls, one of them had been to Emilio breaking their date so he wouldn't be expecting her, either. The flight plan of a small plane flying into Key West could easily get overlooked in the shuffle. It might be days before either she or Gibb were missed.

Days spent alone together on a deserted island with a sizzling sexual energy surging between them.

C'mon. What's wrong with a little sexual thrill? A fling? A hot encounter meant to go absolutely nowhere but give them complete pleasure?

Yeah, it sounded good on the surface, but Sophia

had a sneaking suspicion that a few wild days with Gibb would never be enough. Even now, just thinking about making out with him caused her body to tingle in all the right places.

She grabbed a tool. Must find out what's wrong with the plane. Must get this flying devil back in the air, pronto. Not just to get the impatient Mr. Martin to Key West on time to ruin his buddy's wedding, but to save her own skin. She was not going to, would not, could not have a sexual tryst with him.

A few minutes later, she discovered what had caused the engine to sputter. Whew, it was a minor fix. But her relief was short-lived as she soon stumbled across a bigger problem created by the bumpy touchdown. A problem not so easily resolved. Totally disheartening. Shoulders slumping, she took a step backward and ran smack dab into Gibb.

"Easy." His hand closed around her elbow.

She sucked in air. His body heat surrounded her along with his manly scent. She wrenched away from his grip and scuttled to one side.

Hallelujah, he'd finally taken off his tie and suit jacket and rolled up his shirtsleeves. About time.

Except now, his honed biceps were clearly visible and his muscles were even more impressive than she imagined they would be. He'd also taken off his shoes and rolled his pant legs up to his knees. Sand dusted his toes. On anyone else, it would have looked dorky. But somehow, he managed to still look both stylish and rakishly handsome. Business executive cool 101 or how to dress when crashed on a deserted island.

Seriously, he was too perfect.

An orange sun faded into the dusk as royal-blue twilight crowded the sky overhead. A mosquito buzzed at her ear and she batted it away.

His eyes never left her face.

"What is it?" she asked, unnerved.

He dazzled her with a toothy smile set to "stun" and nodded down the beach at a surprisingly large pile of driftwood with rocks ringed around it to create a fire pit.

Wow. He'd done all that? She was duly impressed.

"Those matches. I need them now," he said.

"Um, sure."

He kept staring at her.

"I'll just go get them out of the cargo hold." She walked backward toward the rear of the plane. She didn't want him looking at her butt again. Why had she worn shorts this short?

His smile never wavered. The breeze ruffled his sandy-blond hair and raised goose bumps over her skin. What would it be like to pull him down in the sand and ravage him? She'd never made out on the beach before, odd considering she came from a country that bordered the sea. But you know what? Out here in the middle of nowhere, she wouldn't mind giving it a go with Gibb.

Knock it off.

She had no choice but to turn her back on Gibb in order to dig the matches out of the cargo hold. She knew, without peeping over her shoulder, that he was still staring at her.

Hormones fluttered inside her like butterflies dancing around spoiled bananas. Her good intentions disappeared with the setting sun. Darkness had a way of making a girl feel so naughty. Why make out on the gritty sand when there was a nice blanket right here in the back of her plane?

Quit it!

Curling her fingers around the lightweight thermal blanket, she closed her eyes. He was a guest at the place where she worked. Hands off, no fraternization with the guests. It was a good gig and she certainly did not want to do anything that would cause her to lose her contract with them.

"Can't find the matches?"

Her eyes flew open. There was Gibb at her elbow looking sexy enough to seduce her without saying a word.

"Here." Her voice was shaky as she passed him the matches.

Their fingers touched.

Talk about igniting the flame. She was almost panting.

His smile said he knew every wayward thought flying through her head because they were flying through his, too. Weakly, she sank against the side of the plane, the blanket clutched to her chest as he strode off.

This time, she was the one to stare at his butt.

6

WITH THE WIND blowing off the water and the sun's vanishing act, the temperature was cooling down. Sophia wrapped the blanket around her shoulders like a shawl and wandered over to the fire pit. Gibb squatted to light an accumulation of dried leaves, sea grasses and twigs. After several minutes of nurturing the fledgling fire, he built it into a crackling blaze.

"Now." He straightened. "What were you saying earlier about cooking something to eat? I'm starving."

"I have a cooler with iced beer, wieners and hot dog buns in the plane."

"You carry wieners with you wherever you go?"

"Not normally, but I was heading over to my friend's house for a cookout after work before you demanded that I fly you to Florida."

"Would this be your male friend?"

"Yes."

"I would say that I'm sorry I interrupted your evening, but I'm not."

What did he mean by that? She glanced up and met his eyes—eyes full of desire.

For her!

Her stomach knotted and she tightened her grip on the blanket. Emilio didn't know yet that they were only going to be friends. She felt so disloyal lusting after Gibb when Emilio was back home unaware. She was absolutely, positively not doing anything with Gibb, no matter how much his sultry looks made her body shiver.

"I'll go get the cooler," she mumbled, ducking her head. Making eye contact with him was dangerous. Already, she felt edgy, achy and the sexual tension increased with every passing second.

"Stay put. I'll fetch the cooler," he said. "You're shivering."

Not from the cold, but from being so near him. "Okay."

He trotted away and for a few minutes she breathed easier until he returned with the red Igloo cooler and she made the mistake of meeting his eyes again.

Whoosh! Five alarm blaze.

From inside of her. Not out.

She'd never experienced anything like this. Not ever. Too bad it was the kind of passion she'd always been searching for. Why did she have to find passion with a wealthy American? She belonged in his world about as much as a biplane belonged in the space program. And in her world, he was just another client, someone for her to fly where he needed to go.

Except right now, they weren't in either of their worlds. This was a strange no-man's-land and that was the problem. No ground rules. No code of ethics. No road map.

Gibb set down the cooler and scanned the area.

"What are you looking for?"

"Something to use to skewer the wieners on."

Sophia burst out laughing.

"What's so funny?"

"You."

"What about me?" He found a dead tree limb and broke off a couple of small branches.

"Never in a million years would I have expected you to skewer wieners."

"Why not? I don't look capable of wiener skewering?"

"Caviar skewering, maybe, but wieners?" She shook her head. Then again, looks could be deceiving. With looks like his, he could have any woman he wanted skewering wieners for him.

"Do you think I have a stick up my spine simply because I have money?"

"Yes, sort of."

"What did I do to lead you to that assumption?"

"You wear a suit. Every single day while you are at a mountain resort."

"I wasn't there on vacation."

"So I gathered from your constant phone calls."

A suspicious expression crossed his face. "You've been watching me."

"I have."

He dropped the tree branches and stalked closer.

She stepped back

His eyes were narrowed. His body tensed.

Her stomach fluttered. Every time he stared at her, it knocked her off-kilter. "What is wrong?"

He moved closer. It was too close. "Are you a spy?"

"Please do not get in my face," she said calmly, even though her knees wobbled.

"Are you a spy? It's a simple question. Yes or no?"

Where was this coming from? What was he talking about? "A spy?"

"You heard me."

"For who?"

"Anyone. Everyone. Fisby Corp."

"Who?" She blinked.

He still hadn't backed off. His face settled into lines. "If you're not a spy, why were you watching me?"

"Are you serious?"

"Deadly."

"Why have I been watching you?" She swept a hand at his clothes. "Look at you. A gorgeous, exciting man in an Armani suit shows up in my quiet little corner of the world and I'm *not* supposed to look?"

A toothy grin broke through the frown and his shoulders relaxed.

"I am not a spy. You are simply…" she paused, searching for the right phrase "…eye candy."

"You think I'm gorgeous and exciting?"

"Oh, please, don't even pretend you don't know you're the sexiest thing on two legs."

He raked his gaze over her. "Look who's talking."

Sophia dug her bare toe in the ground. He said that now, but she could not compete with the likes of Blondie.

"So are we cooking those wieners or not?" She changed the subject. There was already enough tension between them, best to smooth over the spy accusations.

He retrieved the tree branches, skewered the wieners and handed one to her. They sat side by side on the sand roasting the meat and drinking beer.

"Why did you think I was a spy?"

"I'm sorry about accusing you," he said. "I'm jumpy about it."

"Why would someone be spying on you?"

Gibb cast a glance over his shoulder as if he suspected someone was watching them right now.

"Relax," she said. "For better or worse, it's only you and me out here."

"I've been burned by spies twice in two years."

"Fisby Corp?"

"Yes."

"Here, hold this." Sophia handed him her skewered wiener roasted to perfection. She rose up, dusted the sand from her bottom and went to the Igloo chest to retrieve hot dog buns and the squeeze bottle of mustard. "Continue."

"Because I invest in innovative products and entrepreneurs that I believe can earn me a high rate of return on my investments, there are a lot of people who want to copy what I'm doing or even steal from me and the people I've invested in."

"Which is why you wanted me to fly you to Key West instead of summoning your own jet to Libera. Someone could be tracking you."

"Exactly."

She put mustard on the buns and one by one, took the roasted wieners from him, slid them off the tree branches and nestled them into the hot dog buns. She passed one to Gibb, took one for herself and sat cross-legged back down beside him.

For a moment, they ate in companionable silence. It was nice; nothing but the sound of the crackling fire and whispering surf. A half-moon lit the sky.

"These spies are after whatever project you've invested in that's brought you to Bosque de Los Dioses?" she asked.

"That's right. Although to be honest, I can't say there are spies for sure. I've just gotten paranoid."

"Fool me once, shame on you, fool me twice shame on me, fool me a third time and—"

"You've got it." He nodded. "People start questioning my reputation and business suffers."

"But why Bosque de Los Dioses? Why not somewhere else in the world?"

"Costa Rica is well known for its environmentally conscious philosophy. It was a good fit with my project."

"So this is an ecological advancement?"

"It is. Plus the seclusion of Bosque de Los Dioses makes it a perfect place to build our prototype in as much secrecy as possible."

"Except Costa Rica is not known for, shall we say, an aggressive work ethic."

"You have hit the nail on the head in regard to the development issues I've run into."

"This is all very exciting." She rubbed her palms together. "Innovations and spies, high corporate drama going on in my little corner of the world. Can you talk about it at all?"

Gibb hesitated.

"I'm not a spy, I swear." She raised the palm of one hand, put the other down flat like she was pledging on a bible. Her mother had loved courtroom dramas, too.

"I won't get into the details," he said. "It's pretty technical anyway, but I can tell you this much, if the invention works the way the inventor believes it will, it has the potential to revolutionize the way people travel."

"Without oil or gas I'm assuming since it's a green technology."

"Correct. The prototype power source for the special track system will extend from Bosque de Los Dioses to Monteverde, connecting the resort to the nearest village."

"Wait a minute, let me understand this. You're connecting the mountain retreat that is currently inaccessible except by hiking or bush plane to the nearest village, so that people can go up to Bosque de Los Dioses by another means of transportation."

His wide smile brightened his face. "That's right. If everything goes according to plan, we'll be able to—" He broke off. Eyes widening, he stared at her. "I'll put you out of business."

She put a hand to her throat, swallowed hard. "It sounds like it."

Gibb rubbed a palm across his mouth. "Sophia, it never occurred to me that my project would impact your business."

"Why would it?" She shrugged, kept her voice even. What was she supposed to do? She specialized in taking tourists around Cordillera of Tilarán. It was her niche market. There were a couple of other bush pilots in the area, but it was not super competitive.

"It probably won't put you out of business completely," he said. "You might suffer a drop in income, but you can make up for it in other ways."

"You think so?"

He looked uneasy. "Sure."

"You know nothing about my finances. I have to make a certain amount to afford fuel and insurance and upkeep on the plane. That drop in income that you shrug off like it is inconsequential would be enough to ground me."

"There will always be people who want to fly over the mountains," he said. From the expression on his face, he thought this was a lame assurance, too.

"People come to Costa Rica for the ecotourism. Why take a gas guzzling old plane when they can hop on Gibb Martin's spectacular green transportation system." She hugged herself, leaned in closer to the fire.

"It might not even work. The project is a big gamble."

"If you didn't believe in it, you wouldn't have thrown your time and money into it."

"This transportation system will transform the way people travel, Sophia. It will benefit millions."

"And only a few bush pilots will be out of a job."

"It will create more jobs and Costa Rica will be at the forefront of the technology."

He was right. She knew it. Slap a "selfish" label on her. She'd found the one thing in the world she loved more than anything else and the man sitting across from her was putting it in jeopardy.

"I know it's a shock, but you have years to adjust. The track won't even be completed for at least two years, possibly much longer since we're in Costa Rica."

"Score one for me," she said, trying to joke, but it came out sounding sarcastic.

"I'll help you get another flying job. Hell, you could work for me," he said.

"Oh, I'm sure your current pilot would love having a little bush pilot in the cockpit with him."

"You'd need to have more training, of course, but it's a thought."

"I get it. When you run into a problem, you throw money at it and expect it to go away."

Gibb stood up and stalked over to her. He grasped her chin and gently but firmly forced her to look at him. "That's not what this is about."

She wrenched away from him. "It sure feels like it. You tell me your project is going to implode my world and, by the way, here's some money, go get more training and then come work for me?"

"I'm trying to forge a relationship here, Sophia. Between you and me. I made a mess and I want to clean it up. Earlier today you accused me of caring more about my goals than people. I'm trying to show you that's not true."

"Giving me a job to prove you have fantastic relationship skills doesn't make you people oriented. With you, making money will always come first."

"You don't know me well enough to make that assumption."

She raised both palms, got to her feet. "You're right, I don't know you personally, but you've been on my radar for two weeks and I have to say, actions *do* speak louder than words."

"Sophia, I regret that I've hurt you—"

"I'm fine. I'm walking away from this discussion. You're going to do what you're going to do and it's up to me to take care of myself. I'll find an answer on my own. I'm not your problem."

"It doesn't have to be like this. There's a solution."

"I don't want to talk about this anymore." She strode back to the plane. Rich men. *Pfttt.*

She reached El Diablo, rested her head on the wing. She was accusing Gibb of a lot of things, but she had her faults, too. Chief among them, she hated change. Life was easy for her. She was her own boss, set her own hours. She was only twenty-six and owned her own plane. She liked her life and did not want to adjust to a new way of being. In the grand scheme of things, if his project could make life better for many people, she was the one who had to adapt.

Spoiled. She was spoiled. She was the baby of the family and people had indulged Sophia her entire life. Something occurred to her then that had never occurred to her before. Maybe her brothers and sisters weren't as happy as she'd thought about Poppy having given her the plane. Or that she'd been the one he taught to fly. When the others were growing up, he'd been too busy making a living, then too grief stricken once their mother had passed away. Maybe her siblings had kept their opinions to themselves because it was habit, something they just did. Spoil their baby sister.

It had the ring of truth. While she might be adept at sizing up others, when it came to putting herself under the microscope, she looked the other way.

Sophia reached out a hand, stroked one of El Diablo's rivets and murmured, "We could certainly use something revolutionary to travel in now."

"Did you find out what's wrong?"

She let out a startled, "Eek!" She hadn't heard Gibb come up behind her. Stealthy billionaire.

He touched her shoulder. "I didn't mean to scare you."

"I'm sorry for getting upset," she said. "It was just an unpleasant surprise. Like you said, it will take years to build the prototype. Who knows? Maybe by then I will decide to get married, have a big brood and give up flying."

"You'll never give up flying," Gibb said staunchly. "You love it too much."

"You're probably right, but the point is, who knows what the future holds? Things can turn on a peso."

He nodded. "What did you find out about the plane?"

"It was something minor, excess water in the fuel tank. Normally when there is water in the fuel it settles to the bottom and is siphoned out, but fighting that strong headwind sloshed the water around and it accumulated in the carburetor, causing the engine to sputter. All I had to do was drain off the water, problem solved."

Gibb did a little jig that looked so comical on him that she almost smiled. "Great! So we can take off at dawn?"

"Um," Sophia said, hating to break the bad news to him. "Not so fast."

He stopped in mid–happy dance. "What?"

"We hit a palm tree during the emergency landing."

"And?"

"Remember when the plane dropped after we stopped?"

"Yes." He sounded wary.

"A cable on the right rudder broke."

"But you can fix it, right?"

She blew out her breath. "I don't have the proper equipment to repair a broken cable."

"Could you jerry-rig it?"

"Possibly, but I don't know if I can repair it to the level that I trust a jerry-rigged cable to get us very far."

"We could shoot for Island de Providencia."

"With miles of nothing but ocean between here and there. If we have to land in the water…"

He jabbed a hand through his hair. "What else can we do? You said we probably couldn't raise an air tower on the radio."

"No, but when a plane flies over, we can contact them and have them radio for help."

"So all we can do is wait for an aircraft to fly over?"

"Yes. I will still try to competently rig the cable, but I don't recommend holding your breath."

"Either way, it could take days before we're rescued?"

"That's correct."

He muttered a curse word.

"I'm sorry."

"It's not your fault. I'm just frustrated by the circumstances." He pulled a palm down his face.

"You could look at it this way. Maybe the universe is trying to tell you it's time to reevaluate your life."

He stared at her as if she'd suggested he start wearing crystals and chanting "om." She'd merely been trying to help make him feel better about the situation. She wasn't all that happy about being stuck here any more than he was. Her family would be frantic.

"There's absolutely nothing wrong with the way I live my life." He folded his arms over his chest.

"I didn't mean it the way it sounded," she backpedaled. They couldn't seem to have a conversation without conflicting with each other. "I'm not accusing you of anything."

But he wasn't listening. Apparently, she'd pushed one of his hot buttons.

"I'm the American dream," he declared.

"But you're not in America now, are you?"

"I sure as hell wish I were," he said and stalked off into the darkness.

7

HE SHOULDN'T HAVE snapped at Sophia. She'd simply been trying to help him gain a better perspective on things. Gibb knew that. He also knew she was right and that's what irritated him. Lately, his life had taken on a sameness that gnawed at him—work, work and more work. To escape the feeling, he worked even harder, but things seemed to be falling apart. First the spies, then the jam-up on the patent grant and now Scott's defection because he didn't want, in his words, to be consumed by work the way Gibb was.

He was already a billionaire. What was he trying to prove? That he could be richer than everyone?

Being a billionaire wasn't much help to him now when he couldn't even summon a plane to fly him out of here. He paced toward the shore, stared off at the ocean glimmering in the moonlight. Who was he really?

"Gibb?"

He turned to face Sophia.

"I'm sorry, I—"

"Don't apologize," he said. "You weren't wrong."

She was so beautiful standing there, representing everything he did not have—freedom, fun, happiness.

"So all that glitters is not gold?" she whispered.

"I don't have fun anymore. Tonight, cooking hot dogs over a campfire was the most fun I've had since…"

Well, when was the last time he'd had real fun? Sure, he got a thrill from driving his Bentley fast down the Pacific Coast highway, but when was the last time he'd done that? And while it was thrilling, it didn't make him feel like a kid again the way being with Sophia did.

"We seem to be butting heads at every turn," she said.

"I know. I don't want it to be that way. I like you, Sophia. I really do."

She grinned at him. "You want to make s'mores?"

What a smile.

It made him want to lasso the moon, pull it down from the sky and gift it to her on a platinum platter. Except Sophia didn't need all that. She was happy just as she was. How did a person get to be so happy?

She held out her hand to him and he took it. Just like that the fence was mending.

In two minutes they were making s'mores and laughing as gooey chocolate and marshmallows dripped down their chins. Sophia flicked out a delicious pink tongue to lick away the chocolate. Gibb's body reacted instantly and he could not take his gaze from her face.

She caught him watching her. "Oops. That was sloppy."

He moved closer.

Her eyes widened. "What are you doing?"

"Probably making a big mistake," he said.

"Wh—"

But she got no further. He gathered her into his arms and kissed those lips he'd been aching to kiss since the minute he'd first stepped into her plane two weeks ago. He'd ignored the attraction because he'd been with Stacy, but he could deny it no longer. His desire for Sophia was off the charts. It wasn't going to lead anywhere. It couldn't lead anywhere. He didn't have any condoms, but he simply could not go the rest of his life without knowing what it would feel like to kiss her.

Her lips parted and she sank against his chest with a sweet little moan.

Gibb swallowed the sound, swallowed the chocolatey, graham cracker taste of her. Her lips were soft, pliant and sweet. He held her cradled in his arms, exploring her with equal parts of wonder and desire. He felt so alive, so vibrant.

It's just the situation. You're stranded. Alone. It's an adventure. But in his heart, he knew it was more than that. She drew him to her with a magnetic pull he couldn't begin to explain, didn't want to explain in case it ruined the moment.

Hey, he was living in the moment. When was the last time he'd done that? Had he ever done that?

She tunneled her fingers through his hair, clearly enjoying this as much as he was. He had not misread the signals. She was into him, too.

"Sophia," he murmured her name around their joined lips. "Sophia."

Her scent filled his nose, so sultry and feminine. With her tongue she tentatively traced his lips. He met that wicked little tip with his own tongue, sending things moving faster. He pushed past her parted teeth and explored the dimensions of her mouth. The finest wine in the world did not taste this rich, this satisfying.

Gibb's body responded fully, his erection growing hard against her thigh. He could not hide how much he wanted her. In fact, he did not want to hide it.

"Oh," she said breathlessly.

"I'm sorry," he said. "We'll stop. I just couldn't live one second longer without tasting you."

"What if…" She pulled back, her smile wide and inviting. "What if I wanted more than a kiss?"

"Do you?" he asked huskily.

"I… Yes…"

"We shouldn't."

"I know. I have a boyfriend and you have a girlfriend and I'm not a cheater."

"Neither am I, but this thing we're feeling…"

"It can't go anywhere," she whispered. "Not beyond this island."

"Why not?" he asked, feeling suddenly desperate. Why was he feeling so desperate? The need inside him had caught him off guard, stunned him. He couldn't think. All he could do was feel and he wanted to feel what it was like to be inside her.

She laughed.

"What's so funny?"

"I could never be with a man like you. Not for anything more than a good time."

"Why not?"

"*Ticos* are all about family and you are not all about family."

"I could be."

She shook her head.

"Maybe. I've never tried. I want to try with you."

"You are not thinking clearly. You don't even know me."

"I know I want you more than I've ever wanted any woman." His heart was pounding so hard he could barely hear himself speak. Where was this coming from? Why did he feel so out of control? And why did being out of control feel so good?

"You would soon realize I do not fit in your world. Can you imagine taking me to one of your high-society events? I have no idea what's the right fork to use or what to wear in the company of—"

"Do you think I care about stuff like that?"

"You do care about stuff like that."

"How can you say that? You barely know me."

"My point exactly. We hardly know each other."

"What we're feeling has to mean something."

"I think it means we would have a very good time in bed."

"Nothing more?"

She shook her head again.

Why did his stomach feel so hollow? "Where do we go from here?"

"Let's get some sleep," she said in a shaky voice. "As soon as it's first light I will get to work on the plane and see if I can jerry-rig the cable so that it's strong enough to get us to Island de Providencia."

"And then what?"

"You take a plane to Key West to stop your friend from marrying the woman he loves, and I get El Diablo repaired properly and fly home."

"And after that?"

She met his eyes. "There is no after that."

Gibb swallowed. She made good sense. But there

was one problem with that. All his life he'd done the sensible thing. The right thing. On the surface, it had served him well, but it had also brought him here. To this point where he was wondering precisely what his life was all about.

Maybe that's what this feeling for Sophia was. A reaction to the choices he'd made, the realization that without someone to share his life with, all the hard work, all the money in the world didn't mean a thing. Maybe that's why he really wanted to stop Scott from getting married. He didn't want his buddy to find the happiness that had escaped him, because if he did, Gibb would be completely alone. For all these years, he'd dated women who only wanted him for what they could get from him—beautiful women that made for pretty trinkets on his arm but had no substance. And when he met Sophia, he knew instantly that she had substance. She was a woman who made her own living, a woman who was happy in her own skin, a woman who was deeply loyal to those she loved.

He stepped away from her. "Too bad," he said. "I think we could have had something special."

WHAT HAD HE meant by "we could have had something special"? Special sex? Or special something else?

Sophia lay on her back on the blanket beside Gibb, staring up at the starry sky. The fire had burned down to nothing more than warm, glowing embers. She should never have kissed him back, but it had been so worth it. The man could kiss. No doubt about it. Sophia touched her lips.

That was the problem, of course. If he'd been a terrible kisser she wouldn't be awake long after midnight, mulling it over.

She cut her gaze at him. His eyes were closed, his breathing rhythmic. Was he asleep?

What was this special thing? It was lust to be sure, but there was a strong undercurrent of something additional—something deeper, more mysterious than lust. What was it? The feeling wasn't easy camaraderie like what she had with Emilio. Judging from the way Gibb made her feel—hot, breathless, achy all over—it was something far more complicated.

But they'd only been together for twelve hours. What kind of feelings could develop in twelve hours? Sure, they'd been watching each other for two weeks. Covertly flirting with lingering glances and sly smiles, but it had been nothing more than that. These last twelve hours had escalated things between them to an entirely other level.

Maybe it was the crash landing? Emergency situations had a way of bringing people closer together. Maybe that's what this was. They were dependent on each other and had only each other. It created a bond that would otherwise not have been created.

Oh, why had she let him kiss her? She could have stopped it. One palm planted against his chest and a firm "no" would have halted everything. Now, she knew precisely what she'd been missing in the romance department.

A whimper escaped her lips. What had she been thinking? Now she wanted more, more, more.

You weren't thinking. Just like you weren't thinking when you agreed to fly him to Key West.

He'd been staring out to sea, shoulders straight,

hands clenched into fists, and she dumbly walked over to him full of apology and concern.

Instantly, she was afraid he hated her, but when he turned around and she saw that sheen in his eyes, she'd known it wasn't anger. In fact, it was why he was so prickly when he was around her—he was fighting an attraction he didn't want to feel. He didn't dislike her, not at all. In fact, it was the opposite. He'd been turned on.

By her!

He was as taken with her as she was with him. So much so that he'd crossed the line of propriety when Sophia knew he'd never have done so if it hadn't been for being alone on a deserted island. Yes, maybe he shouldn't have kissed her, but she most certainly shouldn't have encouraged it. If she'd drawn a line in the sand, he would have backed off.

Instead, she'd melted in his arms quicker than warmed chocolate and hot marshmallows on a graham cracker.

When his lips met hers, a mist of lust and unbelievable passion had curled around her brain, coaxed her forward into a "what if" dream. What if she were his girlfriend? What if they were to become a couple? What if he was as sensational a lover as he was a kisser? The things he could show her! The places they would go!

Stop it. The dream wasn't real. What was she thinking? He was a billionaire and she was nothing but a simple bush pilot. That kiss had wrecked her reasoning.

Honestly, though, how could she regret that moment with him? She might never be kissed like that again. He kissed the way she wished Emilio kissed. Kissed the way handsome men in telenovelas kissed—deeply, passionately, heartfelt.

Overhead a shooting star crossed the sky and before she knew what she'd done, Sophia made a wish, a wish for so much more than a single kiss.

That's when it occurred to her. Exactly how much trouble she was in. They could be stuck here for as long as a week, with no one else around, nowhere else to go, nothing to do but pretend their sexual attraction didn't exist…surrounded by a hypnotic ocean, the sweet fragrance of jungle flowers.

A week?

If they were here a week there was no way on earth that Sophia would be able to keep her hands to herself. Not when the sexiest man alive was lying right next to her.

STRONG RAYS OF sunlight jerked Sophia awake at dawn. For one disoriented minute, she forgot where she was. Blinking, she sat up, pushed her hair out of her face and rubbed the sleep from her eyes.

Her gaze strayed to the spot beside her and then she remembered—the plane crash, eating s'mores, kissing Gibb Martin, *everything.*

But now, she was alone.

Where was Gibb?

Alarmed, but trying not to panic, she leaped to her feet, searched around for her shoes and found them off to one side of the blanket. She'd lain beside Gibb on that blanket, dreamed of making love to him.

Where had he gone?

Footprints in the sand led toward the forest thicket. Maybe he'd left in search of coconut, bananas or mangos for breakfast. Sophia followed the footprints until they disappeared into the trees.

She stepped past the coconut palms to the green fronds of banana trees and resurrection ferns, past tightly wrapped bromeliads. The farther she went, the thicker the vegetation grew. There were mango trees filled with plump fruit, tall ciebas stretching for the sky, strangler trees and the medicinal smell of eucalyptus. Moss and lichen slicked the forest floor covering the craggy outcroppings of rock.

The jungle was alive with activity. Colorful birds twittered from the trees. She spied a blue-gray tanager, a pair of crimson-fronted parakeets and white winged doves. A bevy of buzzing hummingbirds flitted from one brightly colored flower to another. There were heliconia, pink torch ginger, passionflowers and bougainvillea. Butterflies and moths fluttered about. She recognized thoas swallowtails, a banded peacock, zebra longwings and giant sphinx moths. A red-eyed tree frog stared at her from a banana leaf and she spied a lungless salamander as it scuttled near her feet.

Sophia held her breath. So beautiful! It was an island paradise that rivaled the beauty of Costa Rica. A wave of homesickness hit her and then she heard the sound of water rushing over rocks. A sound she heard every day of her life except for the year she lived in California with her aunt's family.

A waterfall.

The noise drew her deeper into the forest. Maybe Gibb had come into the jungle looking for food, heard the waterfall and decided to make for fresh water.

And even if he hadn't, a quick shower in the cool water sounded heavenly, especially since her hair and clothes smelled like smoke from their campfire.

She trudged through the thick undergrowth. Living

in Cordillera of Tilarán, she was accustomed to the humidity, but the altitude of her volcanic mountain home kept the heat at bay. Here, already, it was at least eighty degrees and the day had only just begun. She longed for the ocean breeze that couldn't reach this far into the dense tropical landscape. But the island wasn't that big. She had to come upon the waterfall soon.

She paused to take a break, plucked a ripe banana from a tree and ate it for energy. Sweat beaded her forehead and she swiped it off with the back of her hand. She resumed her walk, the increasing sound of the waterfall drawing her nearer.

She skirted a strangler tree, pushed through a clump of ferns taller than she was and there it was.

The waterfall.

With a very naked Gibb Martin standing beneath it.

Sophia's mouth dropped open. A punch of pure animal lust hit her low in the belly. He was more magnificent than she'd ever imagined.

His back was to her.

Unbidden, her gaze slid down the full length of his body, starting at the top of his dark head and slipping over the sharp angles and honed muscles of his exquisite frame. His shoulders were broad, his waist lean.

And his butt was so impressive she bit back a whimper of desire. She crouched, not wanting him to see her. She wanted to feast her eyes on him to her heart's content.

She scrutinized the hard planes of his back only slightly obscured by the curtain of falling water. He made a quarter turn, giving her a view of his fine rib cage. Her heart thundered, galloped faster.

He was so athletic and his muscles bespoke hours

upon hours spent at the gym. There was nothing soft about him. He was a rock, strong and stalwart, unmoved by the blasting force of the water.

She shuddered and the most feminine part of her softened, moistened.

He leaned forward, braced his arms on the rock face in front of him, ducked his head and allowed the water to sluice down his exquisite back. The water darkened his sandy-blond hair to the color of refined honey. The glistening strands were plastered sleekly to his head.

Torn between lust and guilt over spying on the guy, Sophia pulled her bottom lip up between her teeth and let out a long, slow sigh. Her blood raced hotly through her veins and the sweat was back on her forehead, but this time it wasn't from the heat.

Her stomach dipped and she took a deep breath. She'd never felt so out of control and she loved the sensation.

And when he turned just a little bit more, giving her a side shot of his rock hard abs, she gasped. She'd never felt pure joy before from looking at a man. She wanted to kiss him from head to toe.

He was wet and smooth and, frankly, beautiful. A work of art.

Compelled by a force that she could not resist, Sophia crept closer, tiptoeing through the thicket of greenery, her pulse pounding through her veins. She trod a thin path along the spongy ground.

The gurgling water churned her erratic thoughts. *Wanna touch him. Wanna stroke him. Wanna taste him. Want him to touch and stroke and taste me.*

The uncontrollable urge to see more of him consumed her. She edged into a small clearing where a beam of sunlight managed to trickle through the tree-tops. She spied his clothes lying neatly folded on a large rock. She resisted the impish temptation to steal his clothes, but oh, boy, just thinking about it had her fanning herself.

His muscles flexed as he washed himself and she simply could not look away.

At last! She had seen him without his suit on. It had definitely been worth the wait.

Head thrown back, face turned up to catch the water flow, eyes tightly closed, he moved and Sophia saw every inch of him in all his naked glory.

And he was totally erect. The man had a lot to be proud of.

Perspiration sweltered on her upper lip. Sophia pressed a palm to her mouth, her breath coming out in short, shallow pants. It was crazy to be this overwhelmed, but she could not pry her eyes off him. A dangerous heat pooled low in her body, spread outward to her limbs in a languid tingle.

Get out of here before he catches you watching him!

Except she could not make herself move and then he did something that sent her over the edge.

Gibb touched himself where Sophia ached to touch him.

Desire claimed her then. Total and complete, and with a force so strong it shoved every other thought, idea, dream and image from her mind. She would not—could not—leave this spot, even if her life depended on it.

_8_

UNDERNEATH THE SOOTHING fall of water, Gibb gritted his teeth and struggled against what his body was urging him to do. He hadn't slept a wink last night. Lying next to Sophia, it had been impossible to sleep. Her body was so lush and tempting, all he wanted to do was touch her, kiss her and make love to her on the sand.

Finally, when he could stand it no longer, he'd risen just before dawn and wandered into the jungle. That's when he'd heard the rushing water and decided to investigate. Maybe exploration would distract him from these ever-present thoughts of Sophia.

After he saw the waterfall, he figured why not use the cold-shower cure? Except that it didn't seem to be working. In fact, all he could think about was what it would be like to have Sophia underneath the waterfall. He shuddered hard as he imagined exactly what it would be like to sink into her sweet body.

He thought about how she'd tasted last night as his lips had claimed hers. How firm her breasts had felt pressed against his chest. How soft her skin had been beneath his palms. How her dark eyes had lit with a hungry fire that matched his own.

She'd captured his imagination in a way no other woman ever had. He was spellbound.

His erect shaft throbbed painfully. If he made love to her, he would cross a line that he'd never before crossed—starting a new relationship before he'd finished an old one. He might be something of a player, but he'd never been a cheater. His stepfather might not have known how to show him love, but he'd drilled honor and integrity into Gibb's head.

Then there was the fact that his head was not in the right place. He was upset over losing Scott as a partner. His need for Sophia might be nothing more than an urge to feel close to someone at a time when everything seemed to be falling apart.

Except deep down, he knew that wasn't true. He would have been attracted to her anytime, any place, anywhere. He found her that compelling.

And that sexy.

She was what he'd been searching for all his life but never dared articulate. If he dared to let himself care for her, she would change him in a hundred different ways.

All of them good.

So what was he afraid of?

Love.

That word. He had no idea what it really meant. But whenever he looked at Sophia, his heart squeezed and he starting thinking *what if?*

You don't know her.

But he wanted to know more. He wanted to know everything about her.

He touched himself, but in his fantasy, it was Sophia's delicate hand rubbing his shaft. Every nerve end-ing in his body sizzled as he imagined cupping her breasts as the water drenched them.

A groan slipped from his lips.

In his mind's eye, he pressed a tongue to the hot pulse of her throat and tasted honey. He brushed his lips against her nipples, felt the pink peaks stiffen. He pressed a hand to her chest, felt the dash of her pulse. He was out of control and he knew it, but he didn't care.

His imagination was so vivid, so real that he could almost hear the sound of her soft moans. "Take me, Gibb. Take me now."

He squirmed, arched his back. His hand moved harder, faster, his thoughts of her, only her, his raven-haired, brown-eyed goddess.

His breath came in short gasps and his brain cried out, "Sophia. Sophia. Sophia."

OH, MY.

Sophia resisted the urge to step forward as she watched Gibb pleasure himself. It was rude, it was voy-euristic, but she found it impossible to look away be-cause it was so incredibly arousing.

Not only did she not look away or leave, but her own hand strayed naughtily to the waistband of her shorts.

What are you doing, Sophia Maria Cruz?

She touched the tip of her tongue to her upper lip and smiled. She was making herself feel better. Scratching an itch. Taking care of this crazy desire in exactly the same way Gibb was.

Once they relieved the pressure, then they could concentrate solely on getting off this island, and they would do it without the messy complication of actually having sex with each other. It was a win-win scenario, particularly when Gibb didn't know that she was in on it with him.

She unsnapped her denim shorts and slid down the zipper. She drew in deep breaths of the thick, humid air and licked her lips.

Gibb rubbed the end of his erection.

Sophia closed her eyes for a second, imagined putting his mouth right where she was touching, drawing moans from her now parched lips. How erotic this was....

She pretended her fingers were Gibb's fingers moving lightly over her skin. Her body ached for him as she continued watching him. He slowed his pace, lengthened the strokes. Mimicking his movements, she pleasured herself long and slow, savoring the damp heat of her body, touching the tender place where she'd imagined he was touching.

"Gibb," she breathed his name on a sigh.

She had hid behind a bush in case he did open his eyes. She didn't want him to get a sudden surprise if he should finish before she did.

It felt so good. She'd never done such an audacious thing, making love to herself in broad daylight out in the open and it felt shockingly free. And yet why not? There was no one to see her, only Gibb.

What would he say if he knew? Would he think it was sexy? Be embarrassed or alarmed at her outrageous behavior. Then again, he had no room to argue, standing up there on that outcropping of rocks underneath the waterfall.

He was her most vivid fantasy come to life.

He quickened his pace, his movements growing frantic.

Sophia followed suit and slipped a caressing finger inside of her hot, wet femininity and a shuddering moan passed over her lips.

Velvet.

A second finger followed the first and she wanted to believe it was Gibb inside her, but no matter how hard she tried, fingers could not approximate a man's taut body. She whimpered. This wasn't working the way she thought it would. It only made her want him more.

She closed her eyes and kept them closed as she thought of his big body over hers. His warm breath on her face and neck. His teasing touch everywhere.

Her entire body tensed. She pinched one of her nipples with her left hand, envisioned Gibb's teeth lightly nipping at her. She arched her back and thrust her hips upward.

Yes, Gibb, yes.

The release was on her, quicker than she anticipated, rocking her body.

Suddenly chagrinned, she grabbed her loose clothing. Her face felt flushed. Her heart rate bounded at a speeding clip. What had she done? Instead of sating herself, her climax only seemed to fuel her desire. She wanted Gibb and nothing short of having him would stop this burning need.

She willed herself to calm down and darted a glance back to the waterfall just in time to see Gibb obtain his own release.

Too bad she hadn't been there to share it with him.

"Sophia," he cried out.

Startled, she jumped, thinking he'd caught her. That

he knew exactly everything she'd just done. Anxiety mixed with excitement as she scrambled to explain herself.

She opened her mouth to tell him she hadn't seen anything, but he sank down on his knees below the rushing water, his eyes still tightly closed.

It dawned on her that he hadn't seen her at all. He'd simply called out her name at his moment of release. While he pleasured himself, Gibb had been fantasizing about her, just as she'd been fantasizing about him.

Emotionally moved, she wanted to go to him, plant kisses all over his face, tell him how excited and honored she was that she was the one that had affected him so. It was humbling and awe inspiring and it made her even more aroused than she'd been before. But she dared not do that.

Instead, Sophia moved away as quietly as she could, praying he did not open his eyes before she disappeared.

FEELING LESS RELIEF than he thought he would, Gibb returned to the beach. He found Sophia working on the rudder at the back of the plane, tools strung out on the ground around her.

"Morning!" he called.

She jumped and looked up, a guilty expression on her face. "Morning," she mumbled, not meeting his gaze.

Good. He didn't really want to look her in the eyes, either. He was still feeling unsettled over what he'd done under that waterfall.

She was breathing fast, too, as if she'd just sprinted a mile in under four minutes, her breasts rising and falling with each accelerated breath. She walked around the left side of the plane.

He followed.

What was she so unnerved about?

Gibb couldn't keep his gaze off her, which was a serious problem. He had to get off this island for so many reasons. He needed to stop Scott from making a mistake. His endeavor back at Bosque de Los Dioses was wide open to corporate spies without him there. But most of all, this attraction to Sophia was getting absolutely out of control. If he stayed around her much longer, he didn't think he could stop himself from seducing her. She was that irresistible.

"I was out scouting for breakfast," he said.

"Oh?"

He pulled fruit from the pockets of his jacket that was still damp from the waterfall spray. "Bananas, mangoes, passion fruit, this place is crazy with passion…" Why did he hesitate after he said the word passion? "…fruit."

"Um, thanks." She dusted off her palms on the seat of her shorts and ducked her head, but not before he saw that her cheeks were bright pink. Was she embarrassed about something?

He thrust a banana at her.

She seemed caught off guard, but accepted the offering.

A steady silence stretched between them as they munched on the fruit. It was not one of those comfortable silences that couples who have been together a long time fall into easily. No, this was one of those edge-of-your seats, sexual tension type silences that seemed to go on forever.

Dammit.

He knew she wanted him as much as he wanted her. That was the central problem. If these feelings were one-sided, then he could have ignored them and the self-pleasuring under the waterfall would have sufficed. But he and Sophia were like two pieces of flint sparking off each other. Sooner or later, they were bound to ignite. All the more reason to get off this island as soon as possible.

"So," they said in unison.

"You go first." He swept a hand at her.

"No, no, what were you going to say?"

"It's not important. What's on your mind?"

"I had nothing of consequence to say, either."

There it was again, that pesky silence.

"I was just…" they said in the same breath.

Gibb laughed. "Okay, one of us is going to have to say what we're thinking."

Sophia looked so alarmed by that comment he had to wonder just what it was that she had been thinking.

"You," she said, "you tell me what you were thinking."

Um, well, he wasn't going *there*. "I was just wondering if you have a better handle on what it will take to repair your plane."

She grimaced. "The cable could be jerry-rigged enough to get us to Island de Providencia, if I could find something to substitute for a ferrule."

"What's a ferrule?"

"It's a cylindrical joint that can be slipped over a cable and crimped to secure it. A thimble would help mightily, too."

Gibb scratched his head. "You mean like a sewing thimble?"

Sophia laughed. "You're not the least bit mechanically minded, are you?"

GET 2 BOOKS

We'd like to send you two *Harlequin® Blaze®* novels absolutely free. Accepting them puts you under no obligation to purchase any more books.

HOW TO GET YOUR 2 FREE BOOKS AND 2 FREE GIFTS

1. Return the reply card today, and we'll send you two *Harlequin Blaze* novels, absolutely free! We'll even pay the postage!

2. Accepting free books places you under no obligation to buy anything, ever. Whatever you decide, the free books and gifts are yours to keep, free!

3. We hope that after receiving your free books you'll want to remain a subscriber, but the choice is yours—to continue or cancel, any time at all!

EXTRA BONUS

You'll also get two free mystery gifts! (worth about $10)

FREE!

He raised a palm. "Guilty as charged. Mechanical as a bumblebee."

"A thimble is a metal sleeve that protects a loop from wear. We could do without the thimble since we're not trying to go far."

"Is there anything on the plane that you can use to fashion into a ferrule?"

"I can't come up with anything I can use as a stand-in. I was about to rummage through the back of the plane and see if that would inspire some creative thinking."

Slowly, she began to unpeel the banana.

His gaze was glued to her fingers. Her movements were so languid and gentle he couldn't help wondering what they would feel like if—

Knock it off, Martin. Stop looking at her hands.

Her lips closed down over the tip of the banana.

To distract himself from the vision, he picked up a plump mango, dried the fruit against the sleeve of his suit and took a bite. The sweet juices filled his mouth, ran down his chin.

Sophia quickly removed a napkin from her hip pocket. She leaned over to dab the juice from his face.

The gesture was so intimate, so unexpected that Gibb's body started to react all over again. How could he get hard again so soon after having an orgasm? Sophia magic. That's all there was to it.

"Thanks," he said gruffly.

She handed him the crumpled napkin and took a step back.

A third elongated silence filled the space between them.

"Would you like to see the broken cable?" she said at last.

As if he could offer any kind of useful input. But it would be something to do besides stand here and feel foolish. "Yeah, sure."

She led him to the rear of the plane and pointed to the rudder. "See here?"

Sure enough, the metal cable had been sheared clean in two. He could not even begin to imagine how she would jerry-rig that. Any lingering hopes he'd had of flying out of here today evaporated.

Don't panic, Scott's wedding isn't until Saturday. It's only Thursday morning. There's still a chance. Slim, but the chance was there. He'd hold on to that hope.

Gibb shook his head. "I can't imagine how you would repair this."

"Let me show you." She found a stick and drew a picture in the sand to illustrate how, if she could find a metal ring of some kind, she could loop it around the cable to secure it in place. "But the trick is that it has to be a piece of metal that I could crimp with pliers or a hammer, while at the same time being sturdy enough to hold the cable closed." She frowned. "I don't think I have anything like that on the plane."

He leaned in and took another look at the cable. In doing so, his elbow accidentally grazed against her breast.

Simultaneously, they both jumped apart.

Sophia sucked in her breath.

"Sorry, sorry. I didn't mean to do that. It was totally an accident."

"I didn't think otherwise."

"That's good because it wasn't otherwise. I didn't intentionally graze your boob."

She chuckled. "Your apology is making things worse."

He cringed. Never mind that his entire elbow was tingling and his blood churned. "It is, isn't it?"

"This is an uncomfortable situation."

"It really was an accident."

"I'm not talking about the boob graze."

"What *are* you talking about?"

She lowered her long, thick eyelashes and sent him a coy smile.

A sudden, disturbing thought ran through his head and somehow he just *knew* that she'd seen him underneath the water. Immediately, his face was hot. He moistened his lips.

He heard a low buzzing sound, like a bee inside his brain. His mind clouded—confused, alarmed, ashamed, he turned away from her.

"Plane," she said.

"What?" He blinked.

She pointed to the sky. "Overhead. It's a plane."

That's where the buzzing was coming from.

Their eyes met.

"The radio!" they cried in unison. What was this tendency they had to say the same thing at the same time?

They raced back to her side of her plane and ran for the door. Their hands landed on the handle at the same time.

They both leaped back as if burned.

Simultaneously, they reached forward again and damn, if their hands didn't collide once more.

"Stand back!" Sophia yelled.

Yes, ma'am. Although it went against his natural instinct, he stepped aside and allowed her to take the lead. This was her plane after all and her radio.

She yanked the door open, hopped inside, put on her headset and fiddled with the dials.

"Dammit," she cried, trying to find the radio frequency of the aircraft that was passing overhead. "Why didn't I have the radio on?"

Gibb blew out his breath, jammed fingers through his hair. Already, he could no longer hear the sound of the plane.

Sophia was speaking into the headset, but he could tell she hadn't made contact, that she was just throwing the information out there, hoping against hope the plane would pick it up.

For several minutes, she repeated her call letters and a mayday message. Finally, in frustration, she yanked off the headset and stormed away from the plane. She stalked to the water's edge and arms akimbo, stared out at the ocean.

"What happened?" he asked, coming up behind her.

"Something's wrong with the radio. I could hear them, but apparently they couldn't hear me. We just lost our only real way of getting off this island."

"IT'S OKAY," GIBB SAID.

Sophia shook her head. "It's not okay. I promised I'd get you to Key West and I failed."

"Look, it's not your fault. You did the best you could. These things happen."

She spun on her heels to face him. "It *is* my fault. I knew better than to try to fly you to Key West in El Diablo, but I let money and a sense of adventure convince me I could do it. Ego. It was pure ego. This is what happens when you get too big for your britches."

Gibb cast a long appraising glance at her body. "You look just right for your britches to me."

"Don't try to make me feel better."

"Why should I kick you when you're down? You're doing a good enough job of that."

"I failed you. I should have turned back the minute I saw those cumulus clouds, but oh, no, I had to be a hotshot."

"I'm the one who pressured you to keep going, remember?"

"I was the pilot." She placed a hand over her heart. "I was the one who allowed you to pressure me."

"Now I see your American side is coming out."

"What do you mean?"

"You're being way too hard on yourself."

"No," she denied. "I'm not being hard enough."

"How's that?"

Sophia raised her chin. "Because there is another reason why I did not want to turn back."

He arched a sexy eyebrow. "What reason?"

"You," she admitted, knowing full well she was treading into dangerous territory.

A smile darted across his face and amusement danced in his gray eyes. He had such remarkable eyes. "Me?"

"I wanted to spend time with you."

"Really?" He said it as if he didn't believe her.

She nodded. "I wanted to be around you since the day I picked you up at the Libera airport. I knew you had a girlfriend, hey, I had a boyfriend, but I didn't care. That's how selfish I was. I wanted to be with you and last night, when you kissed me, I wanted more."

He gulped visibly. "You did?"

"I did. I'm a terrible person, coveting a man I can't have."

"You're not terrible. In fact, you're the opposite of terrible. You're smart and funny and sunny and honest."

"Now you're just trying to make me feel better." But she noticed he did not deny that she could not have him.

"So what if I am? There's nothing wrong with trying to make someone feel better and I am telling the truth."

Sophia drew in a breath so deep it made her lungs shudder. "I'm just so frustrated about all this."

"What?" he asked with a sly grin. "The plane problems or the way you feel about me."

"Both."

"Hey, look at it this way, you wanted to spend time with me, now you get to do a whole lot more of that than if we hadn't crashed."

Her face heated. "I can't believe we're having this conversation."

"How do you mean?"

"I'm supposed to be the laid-back, chilled one and you're supposed to be the hard-driving, let's-get-the-show-on-the-road one. Role reversal."

"It's because we make a good team," he said. "One is up when the other is down and vice versa. We level each other out."

Sophia liked the sound of that. It was true. She couldn't help smiling. "So what do you suggest? Crack open a coconut and lay on the beach and wait for someone to notice we're missing and send out a search party?"

"There is that. I wouldn't have picked this for a vacation, but now that we're stuck here, we might as well make the best of it."

"I can't believe you are saying this. This is such an about-face for you."

"Hey, it's my way of trying to control the fact that I can't control what's happening."

That twisted logic did make sense. Sort of. "It might take Blondie a while to realize you're not back. That black credit card of yours has no spending limit."

"Ah, but your family will sound the alarm."

She frowned, nibbled her bottom lip. "I hate to think how worried my family will be."

"You filed a flight plan. Eventually, we'll be found."

"Yes, but because of the cumulus clouds, I veered off course. It might take quite some time."

"I'm a man of influence. The search party will be aggressive. We will be found." He wasn't bragging, just stating a fact.

"But what about your friend that is marrying the wrong woman? You will not be there to bring him to his senses."

Gibb shrugged. "Maybe it's the universe's way of telling me that I need to let my friend make his own mistakes."

"Can you accept that?"

"What choice do I have?"

"When did you turn philosophical?"

"A day with you is already starting to rub off on me. Wanna go get that coconut?" He winked.

It was tempting. Relax and let nature take its course was the Costa Rican way, but it was a source of pride for Sophia that she would get Gibb to his destination.

"I can't take a break," she said. "I have to go see what happened to the radio. I can't believe the bad luck of a broken rudder cable and a busted radio all because of a little water in the carburetor."

"What's your strategy?"

"Fix the radio first. It's the way we'll most likely get rescued. After I finish that, I'll figure out a way to repair that rudder cable."

"What if I *wanted* you to just hang out with me?"

"I wouldn't believe you for a second. I know what you're really like, Gibb Martin, and it's taking everything you have in you not to tell me to get my fanny in that cabin and fix that radio."

"All right," he said. "I won't stand in your way. But what am I supposed to do while you're working on that?"

"Make yourself useful."

"In what way?"

"Go fishing," she said. "There's only one wiener left, so you might as well use that for bait."

"How do I catch fish without a fishing pole?"

"You're the man who invented Zimdiggy, are you not?"

"I am."

"Then use your imagination." With that, she climbed into the plane and set to work examining what had gone wrong with the radio.

9

USE HIS IMAGINATION, huh? If Sophia only knew how fertile his imagination was, she would not suggest he use it.

Gibb could see her inside the plane, her head bent, her face covered by that jaunty pink hat and his body reacted. Fighting off his baser urges, he took a step forward. He hadn't been fishing in years. About the same length of time it had been since he'd started a campfire.

He reached the door of the plane that she'd left open and peered around the corner. "Can I dig around in your emergency-supply bag?"

"Dig away," she mumbled without looking up at him.

Gibb searched through the canvas bag. He found a bar of soap—wished he'd known that when he took his waterfall shower—matches in a watertight bag, flares, two flashlights and extra batteries, a bag of peanuts, four bottles of water, a Swiss Army knife, candles, a first aid kit and a sewing kit.

Ah ha. Perfect!

All he had to do was braid several strands of thread together to create a fishing line, light a candle, wax up the threads to strengthen the line, bend a sewing needle, tie the line to a stick and bait the hook with the leftover wiener.

An hour later, Gibb cast his makeshift line into the water, where he could already see fish skimming below the crystal-clear water. He lay back in the sand and got comfortable. If someone had told him two days ago he'd be leisurely fishing off a Caribbean island with sewing thread and a needle, he would have laughed. Now, he felt inordinately proud of himself.

A shadow fell over him and he looked to see Sophia standing there.

"What is it?"

"If you're going to lie out here in the sun, you need the hat, not me." She dropped her cowgirl hat down over his face.

The hatband smelled of her hair, sweet, floral, feminine. He pushed the hat up on his face with the tip of his thumb and watched her sashay away. *You can put that swing in my backyard anytime.*

He grinned, settled the hat back down over his face and felt his body relax. He was beginning to see why people took vacations. He must have dozed off, because he jerked awake some time later when the pole he held loosely in his hand gave a tug.

A bite! He had a bite.

Excited, he yanked on the line.

The string pulled tight against him. The fish was big. So big he feared it would break the threads. "Sophia! Sophia!"

She popped out of the plane. "What is it?"

"I caught a fish." It had been so long since he'd been fishing, he forgot what to do.

"Well, pull it in."

"I'm afraid it'll get away."

"Wade out and catch it. You're fishing in shallow water."

"Oh." He hadn't thought about that. He stuck the pole in the ground and bent to roll up the pant legs of his suit. His father would be appalled.

When he finished, he straightened and reached for the pole, only to discover that the fish had pulled it out of the sand and was dragging it out to sea.

"Hey, come back here!" Gibb splashed after the pole and managed to grab hold of it.

But the fish gave another jerk and Gibb fell face forward into the water.

He came up sputtering but still managed to keep his hands wrapped tightly around the pole. "You're not getting away you..."

He and the fish played tug of war for a few minutes, but finally he managed to drag it ashore. It was a good ten-pounder. Feeling as pleased with himself as when he scored a big return on an investment, he slogged back to shore, the flopping fish held triumphantly in his hand.

"Woman!"

Sophia appeared. "You bellowed?"

"Your he-man returns with grub." For effect, he grunted like a caveman.

Her eyes crinkled at the corners when she smiled. "You look all of twelve years old."

"What a rush! It was amazing." A pump of endorphins lit him up like the Las Vegas strip. The morning was warm, but he was wet. He shivered. From the damp or from something far more complicated? "What kind of fish is this?"

"Snook."

"Is it edible?"

"Delicious."

"Ha!"

"I like seeing you this way." She canted her head and studied him with an expression that made his entire life up to this very moment worth living. The look was filled with so much more than sexual attraction. It was beyond friendship. It was bigger, richer, fuller, magnified, leaving him tongue-tied and speechless.

How incredibly beautiful she was with her glossy black hair shining in the sun. Her smile dug deep down inside him and for one moment Gibb felt a sudden urge to turn and run, but there was nowhere to go. Besides, he was filled with wonder and awe. And he might as well admit it, fear, because these kinds of thoughts did scare a guy, didn't they? And Sophia stirred all kinds of crazy feelings inside him.

It wasn't just that her dark brown eyes seemed to shine brighter. It wasn't that her breasts were pert, poking through her bra and that devastating little crop top. It wasn't even her flat, taut, caramel-colored belly that he tried not to pointedly stare at. The unbelievable part was that in the short time they'd been apart—her working on repairing the radio, he fishing—he missed her. Sophia seemed to have taken on a lustrous, incredible glow that he hadn't noticed before. Who had changed? Him or her? Or maybe they both had?

"Sophia." He breathed.

"Yes?"

"You look…" He couldn't think of a word to fit her image, but he sure was staring.

She stood barefooted, sand covering her sexy little

toes painted a pearly peach color and she put a hand to her cheek. "Do I have something on my face?"

He shook his head, opened his mouth to tell her she was the most gorgeous creature he had ever clamped eyes on, but no words came out. The craven urge to run overtook him again but even if he could have sprouted wings, he couldn't fly. His feet were rooted to the spot, ground deep like a thousand-year-old sequoia.

And if the gasping fish hadn't flopped against his leg, Gibb could have stared at her until the end of time.

"You're sopping wet," she said. "Strip off."

"Wh-what?" he stammered.

"Out of those clothes." She snapped her fingers. "Take them off. Now. You'll catch your death of cold."

He started to argue that being wet and cold didn't cause illness, but why miss an opportunity like this? "Strip off everything?" He grinned slyly.

Her cheeks colored. "Um, keep your underwear on, of course. They will dry fast in this heat. I'll spread your suit out on the airplane's wing for the sun."

"What do I do with this?" He held up the fish.

"Here, give me that." She took the fish from him, holding it by the line. "Off with the clothes."

"Yes, ma'am." He'd shrugged off his wet jacket.

She held out her free arm and he draped his jacket over her elbow. There was no mistaking the lusty look in her eyes. No doubt about it. This woman would be very responsive in bed, or on the ground for that matter.

His fingers went to the buttons of his shirt. "I feel so cheap," he teased.

She snorted and turned her head, but a second later, he caught her eyeing him again.

He started humming, "The Stripper," as he finished unbuttoning his shirt and whisked it off. When he stepped forward to drape the shirt over his jacket on her arm, he saw she was trembling.

Truth be told, so was he.

"What happened to your chest!" she exclaimed.

Gibb put a hand to the puckered puncture wounds in the center of his sternum. "Stingray."

"My gosh. Like the Crocodile Hunter?"

"Exactly like the Crocodile Hunter," he confirmed.

"When did it happen?"

"Ten years ago. My buddy and I were diving off the Great Barrier Reef."

Sophia hissed through clenched teeth. Her concern touched him. "How did you manage to survive being barbed in the chest?"

"Through the quick thinking of my friend Scott."

"The guy whose marriage you want to stop?"

"Yes." Gibb rubbed the scar. It didn't hurt anymore, but the memory of that intense pain still lingered. "If Scott hadn't been there to stop me from pulling the barb out, I would have likely died. It's a natural instinct to want to pull it out."

"Scott saved your life."

Gibb nodded. "Because of the medical training he'd received in the Coast Guard, he knew just what to do."

"And now you believe it's your turn to save him?"

"Well, despite what I said earlier, marriage isn't quite life or death, still, I have to make sure he knows what he's getting into."

"You must have suffered a great deal."

"No biggie." He shrugged. Honestly, he didn't really like talking about it. To derail the conversation, he unsnapped the fastener on his pants.

Her gaze drifted lower, following the movements of his hand.

Gibb eased the zipper down. Teasing her a bit, but it backfired. He was aroused and the minute he took his pants off she was going to know exactly how much he wanted her.

She seemed to catch on and quickly turned her back to him. "Hurry," she said in a husky voice. "I don't have all day."

"Um, could you back up here so I can use your shoulder to help me balance while I strip my pants off. When they're wet, they stick to skin."

"So I've noticed," she mumbled as she backed up toward him, her arms outstretched, fish held in one hand, his clothes in the other.

"You know," he said, resting his hand on her shoulder. "This could be a sitcom episode."

Her muscle twitched beneath his palm. *"Gilligan's Island."*

"I'd be the professor," he said, balancing on one leg as he peeled off his soaking-wet pants.

"Not hardly. You're Thurston Howell the third."

"Hey," he protested, shifting to the other leg. "I'm not that old."

"Okay, I'll give you that. Mr. Howell was older, but you've got the same outlook on life—money, money, money. Plus, he was a dapper dresser just like you."

"That's stereotyping."

He tugged off the other pant leg. The warm breeze hit his wet skin and the erection he'd been working on stiffened. Good thing her back was to him. He was also glad he preferred boxers to briefs, although more than one girlfriend had made fun of him for that. Calling him old-fashioned. Hey, his underwear was pure silk and cost a hundred dollars a pair. Once you've had that kind of luxury, it was hard to go back. Oh, god, he *was* like Thurston Howell the third.

"Be happy that I didn't say you reminded me of Gilligan or the Skipper," Sophia pointed out.

"I suppose I should take my strokes where I can get them."

The word "strokes" seemed to hang orphaned in the air. Or maybe it was just his imagination since he'd been dreaming of stroking Sophia in a thousand different ways.

"So who am I on the island?" she asked. "Mary Ann or Ginger?"

"Hands down, Mary Ann."

"Why Mary Ann?"

"Are you kidding me? Petite, dark hair, spunky." He added his trousers to the pile of clothes on her arm and took the fish from her. He held the snook up in front of him to block her view of…ahem…down under in case she should face him.

"And cute as a button," Sophia said with disdain.

"What's wrong with cute?"

"Why not Ginger? Why don't you see me as Ginger?"

He felt caught off guard by the question. Why would she even want to be Ginger? Mary Ann had substance. Ginger was all flash. "She has red hair."

"That's superficial. What if Ginger had black hair? Could I be Ginger then?"

"Ginger would never have black hair."

"But what if she did?"

"Ginger is tall."

"So what? Height is not everything."

"Are you getting mad at me?"

She turned around, her nostrils flared. "What's Ginger got that I don't have?"

"Nothing! That's what I'm trying to tell you."

"Just once," Sophia said. "I'd like to be sexy and slinky like Ginger."

"Believe me, sweetheart, you're plenty sexy," Gibb said.

"Blondie is a Ginger, isn't she?"

"Stacy? Yeah, she's a Ginger."

"See, even you like Ginger better."

"I do not like Ginger better."

"Then why are you with her?"

"Why, Sophia, are you jealous?"

She tossed her head back, sending a cascade of black hair rippling over her shoulders. "I wish I was tall and slinky."

"Don't get me wrong, Ginger has her place, but Mary Ann?" Gibb shook his head. "She's the woman you want by your side when the chips are down."

"The chips are down now," she said.

"They most certainly are."

Sophia looked pleased and he wanted to laugh out loud with joy that he'd pleased her. "Go take care of the fish," she said. "I will spread your clothes out to dry."

"I'm on it."

As Sophia walked away, Gibb couldn't help thinking that neither Mary Ann nor Ginger could hold a candle to her.

"YOU ARE A very good cook," Sophia announced over a late lunch of grilled snook and mangoes.

Gibb sat across from her on a rock wearing black silk boxers. It was all she could do to keep from sneaking glances at him.

"Mmm. This is delicious," she carried on.

"I'm a man of many talents," he bragged.

"Humility not being one of them," she teased.

He winked at her.

Sophia's body heated and she got so flustered, she couldn't hold his gaze. Whatever was going on with them seemed to have escalated by warp speed. Probably because he was nearly naked and his honed, muscled chest was on display right there in front of her. She had a strong urge to run her tongue over the irregular edges of his scar.

"I repaired the radio," she blurted because she couldn't take any more of this flirtatious banter or how his silk boxer shorts flattered his legs. She was hanging on by her fingernails here.

Gibb's eyes brightened. "Excellent. I knew you could do it. What was wrong?"

"A cable inside the radio got crimped, I'm guessing during the course of the bumpy landing. I had to take the entire radio apart to find what it was but once found it was a quick fix. All I had to do was uncrimp the cable. We're good to go the next time a plane flies over."

"That's a step in the right direction."

"Next problem to solve is the rudder."

"Is there enough light left to tackle that today?"

Sophia eyed the sky. It was three o'clockish, not even twenty-four hours had passed since they'd touched down on the island. "It's not the light that's the issue. We have the campfire and flashlights. The main issue is that I still haven't come up with a possible replacement for a ferrule."

She had racked her brain trying to think what she could use as a substitute. "If only there was some kind of linkage, a chain—"

An idea started to form. It was illusive at first, but in her mind she kept seeing a link. Mentally, she chased after the image trying to remember where she'd seen such a thing.

"Sophia?"

"I've got it!" She jumped to her feet.

"Got what?"

The platinum bracelet that Gibb wore was perfect. She could dismantle it, take out two links from the chain, position the broken cable through the links and hammer the chain so hard around the cable that the forged metal wouldn't allow the cable to separate in flight. At least long enough to get them to the Island de Providencia. Of course, that meant destroying what was undoubtedly an expensive piece of jewelry. Her gaze flew to his right wrist.

It was bare.

"Where is it?"

"Where's what?"

"That chain you wear around your wrist. If I take out a couple of links, they'd do as a makeshift ferrule. Where is the bracelet? You had it on last night."

Gibb's hand went to his wrist and he muttered a curse.

"Did it come off in the water while you were fishing? Let's go look for it."

"No." He shook his head. "I took if off this morning when I showered beneath the waterfall. It must still be there."

An extra blast of heat went over Sophia as she remembered that morning at the waterfall. She ducked her head so her eyes would not give her away. Suddenly, her body ached exactly as it had when she'd spied on him.

"Let's go find it," she said, charging ahead of him into the jungle, but then made herself stop. She didn't want him to know she knew where the waterfall was. If he ever found out she'd seen him...

He came up behind her.

"Which way?" she asked, hoping her nose would not grow from feigning ignorance.

He took her elbow. "This way."

She dissolved at his touch. His bare chest was so close. All she'd have to do was reach out a hand and she could strum his defined ribs with her fingertips. A jolt of awareness electrified her. They were about to return to the scene of the crime so to speak.

Gibb went ahead of her. The thin path through the thick foliage was too narrow for walking abreast. He pushed aside thick fronds, held them back until she'd passed by them. The waterfall pattered, the sound drawing them closer to it.

She ran her gaze over his naked back. He was all sinew and muscles, straight out of a fantasy. She thought about the scar on his chest and she imagined stroking it with her fingers.

The silk boxer shorts flowed like water when he moved, dark and silky. It made her think of dark nights and naughty deeds. Everything about him, from his intelligent gray eyes, to the sleek way he made her feel privileged to be in his extraordinary company.

That was the problem of course. A woman like her would never be in the company of a man like him outside of a plane crash on a deserted island. *This* was fantasy. She knew that, did not believe that it could ever be anything more. As long as she kept that straight, anything that happened between them would be fine.

Her gaze strayed down his spine to the waistband of his boxer shorts. The air fairly vibrated with his masculine energy and it stirred the thick sexual undercurrent that had been brewing between them for the past two weeks.

The sound of the waterfall grew nearer. The afternoon sun peeped through the trees here and there, casting long shadows through the jungle.

Gibb turned slightly, held out his palm.

He wanted her to take his hand?

Thrilling, absolutely thrilling, and scary to boot.

He wriggled his fingers at her.

Sophia accepted his hand and allowed him to lead her deeper into the forest. His grip was firm, warm. She felt secure in a way she'd never quite felt before. It was a fairy tale. Surreal.

Keep your mind on what you're doing. Get that bracelet, get back to the plane, work as fast as you can to repair that cable and you might be able to get out of here before sunset.

And before she completely gave in to temptation.

Her breath was already coming out labored in the humid air. It felt as if they were moving languidly through water. Time crawled as she became infinitely aware of everything—the feel of Gibb's palm pressed against hers, the way the rippling muscles in his arm stood out, how she and Gibb seemed to be connected by so much more than just their hands.

The waterfall became louder, along with the pounding of Sophia's pulse as she recalled exactly what she'd done that morning when she'd watched Gibb. Heat swamped her.

He parted the fronds in front of them and there it was, the waterfall, bathed in a swath of sun as colorful birds flitted through the sheltering trees. A shimmering rainbow glowed at the top of the fall, several feet above their heads. Cooling spray splashed her heated skin. Her gaze went to the spot on the opposite side of the pool where his clothes had been left folded on the closest rock.

Gibb's hands tightened around hers and Sophia's stomach dipped and swirled. Was he reliving this morning's events, as well? She held on to him. The lusty part of her was hoping for a kiss.

But Gibb simply stopped, his eyes narrowed. Sharp, smart eyes that missed nothing. Intense eyes that belied his youthful age. He was accustomed to being cautious, guarded.

Metal glimmered in the yellow light.

"There it is!" she exclaimed. Salt. Disappointment tasted like salt in her mouth. Had she not wanted to find the bracelet? Sophia shook off the thought. No way. She was happy. Elated. Ready to get off this island in fact. Ready to be on her way.

"Where?" he asked.

"Right there." She pointed.

"I don't—"

But before Gibb could finish speaking, a black and brown spider monkey scampered down from a strangler tree, snatched up the bracelet with one hand, and with the toes of one of his long back legs swung away on a vine like Tarzan.

10

"GET THAT monkey!" Sophia shouted.

Gibb was already on it, tearing through the dense foliage, Sophia on his heels.

The monkey chattered, apparently enjoying the game.

"Come back here," Gibb yelled.

The monkey grinned wide, flashed a row of teeth and dangled the bracelet a few feet above Gibb's head, taunting him.

Stretching his arm wide, Gibb jumped up, tried to snag the bracelet from the monkey's paw. Futile. He knew it. But Sophia was watching.

The monkey let loose with a gleeful noise and leisurely reached out with his other paw and grabbed another vine. Two quick swings, and he vanished from their sight.

"Dammit!" Gibb swore.

Sophia giggled.

"It's not funny." He glowered.

She slapped her hand over her mouth and struggled

to look serious. "The situation is not funny, but you swearing at a monkey makes me smile."

"Well," he said sheepishly, "I'm glad I amuse you."

"Also, when you jump…"

"Yes?"

"You, um…jiggle."

He put a hand over his private parts. "You weren't supposed to be watching that."

A mischievous light sparked in her eyes. "Now what woman would not be staring at a guy with a fit body like yours?"

Not to be outdone, Gibb raked his gaze over her body. She sure filled out those shorts.

Sophia was the first one to look away. She moved ahead of him, pushed back fronds and vines and charged heedlessly into the forest. "C'mon."

"Get real," he called after her. "We don't stand a chance of catching him."

"I don't know about you, but I'm not a defeatist. Think positive."

"Okay, I'm positive we don't stand a chance of catching him."

The monkey chattered up ahead, unseen among the leaves.

"See, he's laughing at us. He knows we're up a creek without a paddle."

Sophia kept going, her curtain of long black hair swaying against her waist as she moved. What an image. It only took her a few steps and she was out of sight, too.

"Hey, wait up," he said, rushing after her. The verdant air smelled of spoiled fruit. Gibb stepped on a rotten mango and it squashed messily beneath his foot.

Ugh. He swiped his foot against moss growing on a tree root. He felt as if a hundred pairs of luring eyes were watching, sizing him up as a potential meal.

The tropical forest was Sophia's territory, not his. Give him a boardroom or a cocktail party over a wild jungle and jewelry-stealing monkeys any day of the week. That platinum bracelet had cost him five thousand dollars, but money wasn't the issue. The real value of the "gent's band" as the jeweler in Australia had called it, was what it represented—his bond with Scott.

Yes, the infernal jungle was unpleasantly sultry and the monkey was annoyingly irritating, but what about the rainbows and waterfall and fishing and campfire s'mores? Had to take the good with the bad, right?

He followed the leaves still trembling from her recent passage. Vines and twigs scraped his body. He wished he had on more than silk boxer shorts and Gucci loafers. He stepped over fallen trees, skirted an anthill crawling with black ants so big they looked like licorice jelly beans with legs, tread carefully over soft ground and startled when he almost touched a long green snake so camouflaged he didn't see it until its quick red tongue flickered at hm.

"Sophia?" Gibb called out. Where had she gone?

"Shh," she hissed.

Slowly, Gibb inched forward through the vegetation. After some minutes, he found her standing perfectly still in a small clearing.

"What is it?" he whispered.

Sophia pointed upward.

The spider monkey that had stolen his bracelet was perched high in the top of a tree and sitting beside him on the branch were two other monkeys.

Gibb craned his neck. "All right, you found him. What now?"

She tapped her forehead. "Let me think."

The platinum glimmered in the sunlight. One of the other monkeys scooted closer to the first monkey and tried his best to look completely nonchalant.

"Maybe if we could tempt them with some fruit..." Sophia mused, stroking her chin with her thumb and forefinger.

"They've got fruit all around them. Why would they come down here where we are?"

"You got any better ideas?"

He did not.

Suddenly, the second monkey made a grab for the bracelet. The first monkey screamed and shoved the second monkey who slipped from his perch. He chattered angrily at the first monkey, snatched up a vine and swung to a nearby tree.

"A day at the zoo," Gibb muttered.

"Have you ever been to the San Diego Zoo?"

That seemed a random reference. "Sure. Have you?"

"My aunt Kristi took me there many times while I lived with her. I think she thought that seeing all the animals would keep me from being homesick."

"Did it? Keep you from being homesick?"

Sophia shook her head.

"It had to be hard for you so far away from home when you were so young."

She kept her eyes trained on the monkeys, but her shoulder muscles tensed. "It was fun, too, playing with my cousins. I missed them when I returned to Costa Rica."

"How long did you live with your aunt and her family?"

"A little over a year." She shifted her weight from one foot to the other.

It was clearly a tender topic and he wasn't sure why. He should probably stop quizzing her, but she was so fascinating that he wanted to know everything about her. "How was it that you came to live with your aunt's family?"

She paused for so long that he thought she wasn't going to answer. "Never mind," he rushed to say. "It's none of my business."

"My mother died of bacterial meningitis when I was twelve."

"Ah, Soph, I'm so sorry." Now he felt like a jerk for being nosy. "That had to be tough."

Sophia shrugged, but her eyes were sad. "It was a long time ago, but I still remember that zoo. I loved the monkeys most of all because they were so much like people."

"Funny," he said, "that you liked the zoo when you were raised among animals in the wild."

"Here's the thing. I took my home for granted until I went to the zoo. It was only then that I recognized that not everyone was as privileged to see these beautiful creatures in their natural habitat. Going to the zoo made me feel so very lucky and I'm thrilled there was such a wonderful place for people to come and see animals that they might otherwise never have the chance to see." Her face took on a pensive quality that made him feel as if he were the most deprived man on the face of the earth.

"I get it, Soph."

The first monkey stuck the bracelet in his mouth.

He bit down on it, took it out of his mouth, studied it and then bit on it again as if testing to see if it was real. A third monkey closed in on the first. This one wasn't playing coy. He was clearly intent on getting his hands on the bracelet. He puffed up his chest and made quarrelsome noises that Gibb imagined was something along the lines of "hand it over, buddy," in primate speak.

The thieving monkey bared his teeth at the third and held the bracelet behind his back like a kid playing keep away. The second monkey popped back up again behind the first monkey while he was fending off the third monkey.

The second monkey snagged the bracelet and took off, making a deriding noise.

The monkey who'd originally made off with the bracelet let out a shriek and the chase was on. Three monkeys swung and shook the trees, jabbering at each other like trash-talking professional boxers.

"Why do I feel like I'm on an episode of *Punked?*" Gibb mumbled.

Sophia elbowed him in the ribs. "Keep moving. If they get away we have no chance of getting that bracelet back."

Not knowing what else to do, he followed her once more. "You are clearly an optimist, Sophia Cruz."

"I can't believe you are such a pessimist," she tossed over her shoulder as she plunged deeper into the jungle. "As successful as you are, I thought you would have learned by now that you have to see past external appearances in order to achieve goals. Just because all seems lost doesn't mean that's the case."

"It sounds like you're speaking from experience."

"When my father gave me El Diablo everyone

laughed at me. No one except my father thought I could make a go of a bush charter service."

"How did that make you feel?"

"More determined than ever. I am very headstrong when I set my mind to something. Besides, I had Poppy on my side. All it takes is one person to believe in you."

The way that James had believed in him. His adopted father might not have been demonstrative or ever told Gibb that he loved him, but he'd set the bar high and held Gibb to that standard.

"It wasn't easy," she went on. "El Diablo was not in the best shape. The plane had been grounded for over a year before my father finally came to terms with the fact he was never going to fly again."

"That couldn't have been easy for either one of you."

"I remember the day Poppy came to me and said, '*Mi, hija,* I have been a vain man, unable to admit when my race is run, but it is not right for a beautiful bird like El Diablo to stay grounded simply because I am. It is his destiny to fly and you are the one I want to fly him.' Then he gave me the keys and hugged me and we both started crying."

"I can't get over the amount of courage it took for you to succeed in spite of the naysayers."

"'Daydreamer,' they all called me. 'Just like your mother.' But they did not know that daydreaming is how you see the big picture. I looked past the obstacles, fixed my gaze on my goal and went after what I wanted." She cocked her head and grinned. "That, plus I've read *Jonathan Livingston Seagull* like nine hundred times."

"You have an amazing spirit, Sophia Cruz." He heard the admiration in his voice, acknowledged he did admire her deeply.

"So take a page from my notebook and believe that we can get that bracelet back."

"There's optimism and then there's pipe dreaming."

"But how do you know it's only a pipe dream until you try?"

"I'm optimistic when things are within my control," he said. "When things are out of my hands…then that changes the playing field."

"You can never tell when the tide will turn."

Gibb slogged through the dense underbrush. His feet kept slipping on the slick lichen and the silk boxers were swishing against his thighs, causing a friction rub. "I could do with a turning tide right about now."

Sophia disappeared from his view again. Damn, he better pick up the pace if he didn't want to get left behind in the jungle. He wished he had his phone to use the GPS. He shoved aside a banana leaf and she wasn't there. It would be so easy to get lost in here. One big green frond looked pretty much like another.

"Sophia? You there?"

No reply.

"Soph?"

Well, he'd be lying if he said his pulse hadn't kicked into overdrive. What if something had happened to her? Disturbing images of a jaguar snatching her up in its jaws raced through his head, but when Sophia reached out a hand from the overgrowth, slapped her palm over his mouth and pulled him up beside her, what he felt was—

Utterly aroused.

Her soft breasts were pressed against his back, her palm tasted both sweet and salty against his lips and her elbow was crooked around his neck. Her sexy scent invaded his nostrils, fanned the flames burning inside him.

"Don't say a word," she whispered in his ear, her voice low and her breath warm and ticklish against his skin.

Silk boxer shorts didn't disguise a thing. Gibb closed his eyes, gritted his teeth and fought a losing battle against nature. The only saving grace? She was behind him.

"They're close to the ground." She removed her hand from his mouth.

Who? What? Huh? What was she talking about?

Chattering and rustling came from the nearby trees.

Oh, yes, the monkeys. Gibb opened his eyes.

Just inches above their heads sat the three monkeys playing tug-of-war with the bracelet.

"Don't move," she murmured. "They're so busy fighting that they haven't noticed we're here."

They stood like that, not moving, Sophia's lush body pressed to him. At this point, he was so worked up that he didn't give a damn about the bracelet. Which, considering he'd worn it every day for the past ten years, was saying something.

The spider monkeys swatted at each other, slapped and bickered.

"Monkeys are interesting," he observed, determined to get a handle on his desire by grabbing hold of anything that could shift his attention.

"They are," Sophia concurred.

The monkey who currently had the bracelet jerked his head up, spied them, let out a screech and took off through the trees, the other two hot on his trail.

"Come on," Sophia said. "Let's go."

Gibb groaned. "How long are we going to do this?"

"Until we get that bracelet back." The grit in her voice spoke of the kind of determination it took to be a venture capitalist.

He smiled. "Let's get it, then."

They were so deep into the forest now that no sunlight filtered through. Everything was shaded and shadowed and the air was distinctly cooler. From far behind them came the faint roar of the waterfall. They'd been out here for hours. Even if by some miracle they managed to get their hands on the bracelet now there was no way Sophia could repair the plane in time to fly out of here before sunset. Another day. They'd lost another whole day, but sometimes admitting defeat was the best plan of action.

He was just about to say this, when the miracle happened.

The monkey dropped the bracelet—plunk—right there at Sophia's feet. She snatched it up with a triumphant hand. "Got it."

The monkey screamed and started jumping up and down on the branch. His cohorts joined in.

"You snooze, you lose," Sophia told the monkeys and slipped the bracelet into the front pocket of her shorts.

One monkey snatched a passion fruit from a tree and chucked it at them.

"Hey!"

The second monkey joined in, then the third.

It was a monkey melee as they pelted Gibb and Sophia with passion fruit.

"Ouch!" Sophia raised an arm to protect her face. "Vicious little freaks."

"C'mon." Gibb grabbed her hand. "Let's get out of here."

Laughing, they ran through the trees, sticky with passion-fruit juice. Once they were out of range of the ill-tempered simians, they stopped running and paused to catch their breath.

"Boy, are monkeys sore losers," she muttered.

He met her gaze and they started laughing all over again.

"You've got stuff on your ear," he said, leaning in to flick away the glob of fruit seeds with his thumb.

She stared deeply into his eyes and he had the sensation that he was falling into her welcoming arms.

"What now?" he murmured.

"I don't know about you, but I need to rinse off. Let's see if we can retrace our steps and find the waterfall."

Gibb glanced around them. "How can you retrace your steps in the jungle? I mean, plunk me down in Manhattan or Miami or Paris and I'm your guy. But this place?" He shook his head. "Your bailiwick."

"We'll try to follow the sound of the water. If worse comes to worse, we'll eventually find the ocean. This is an island, after all."

"Lead the way."

It was odd, being the follower for once. He was normally a hard-charging dynamo, rampaging from one project to another. But he wasn't too proud to admit when he was out of his league.

They tramped through the jungle for what seemed like hours but was probably no more than thirty minutes. He was more than ready to get back to the beach and into some clothes.

The vegetation started to thin and the sound of the

waterfall was growing louder when Sophia stopped so abruptly, Gibb almost plowed into the back of her.

"Look," she said breathlessly. "Oh, Gibb, just look!"

He peered over her shoulder to see what she was pointing at, but he was too distracted by her scent to pay much attention. Her breathing was coming in quick little inhales and exhales of air, her sensual lips were parted, her gaze transfixed, the blue vein at the hollow of her throat pulsed rapidly.

She was excited.

And her excitement excited him. Everything about her turned him on.

"What is it?" he asked.

"Ghost orchids," she whispered.

"Huh?" Finally, he wrenched his gaze from her and looked to see what she was talking about. Dazzling white flowers hung suspended from a thin network of vines wrapped around the base of a number of bald cypress trees.

"One of the rarest orchids in the world," she said. "Do you know how special this sighting is?"

"Pretty unique?"

"It's a once-in-a-lifetime find." Legs shaking, she edged forward. "The ghost orchid."

Gibb examined the flowers with new respect. Anything that had the power to reduce tough little Sophia to trembling deserved his reverence.

The luminous white flowers had no leaves and hardly any stem. In fact, they seemed to be suspended in mid-air. He'd never seen flowers shaped quite like this. They resembled albino frogs with long legs extended.

"Magic," Sophia murmured, running her fingertips over the slender petal. "Pure magic."

As the twilight deepened, the flowers took on an ethereal glow. From the shadows descended a flurry of giant moths almost as big as hummingbirds. They fluttered about, from flower to flower, hungrily drinking sweet nectar.

"I can't believe we are lucky enough to be here to witness this! Amazing. Sharing this moment with you is something I will remember for the rest of my life."

She was going to remember him for the rest of her life? Exaltation swelled Gibb's chest, made him catch his breath. Impulsively, he reached for her hand, squeezed it.

For the longest time, they stood there, holding hands and watching the flying ballet. Breathing in the calliope of fragrance—an effervescent aroma, fresh and clean with undertones of grapefruit, moss, vanilla and the barest hint of star anise. The hot, steamy jungle night enfolded them. Insects chirped. Unseen creatures rustled through the foliage. The queenly orchids glowed, beguiling beacons in the sultry darkness.

Suddenly, Sophia giggled.

"Wanna share?"

"The nickname of the sphinx moth." She kept giggling.

"What is it?"

"The flying tongue."

"Oh, ho?" He grinned at her.

"Only the sphinx moth can pollinate the ghost orchid. They have six-inch tongues."

"Only six inches?"

She giggled again. "Trust a man to make that comment. The sphinx moth follows the scent of the ghost orchid like bees involved in a pollen orgy."

"That's erotic imagery." He was already aroused.

"The ghost orchid is erotic," she purred.

He lowered his lashes, studied her through the fringe.

Sophia spun in a half circle. Like a sprite among the sexy jungle plants, arms extended wide, she lifted her face to stare up at the thick canopy of trees and murmured again, "Magic."

Gibb could not take his eyes off her. Yes, yes it was. Magic unlike anything he'd ever experienced. He had to agree. The scent was as intoxicating as the finest wine. It swelled and surged on the night breeze like symphony music, a heady rush of exuberant notes.

Sophia had stopped spinning and was staring at him now with heavy-lidded eyes. Gibb caught his breath, knew she felt it, too—this headlong craving to be joined.

He gave her the most sensuous look he could muster and the one she sent him in return smoldered with sexual intensity. He aimed a notorious smile at her.

Her answering grin was just as deadly, reaching straight through to his heart.

What a woman—sexy, beautiful, compelling! He loved the way she loved life. He thought he'd known how to enjoy what he had. He drove fast cars, dined in four-star restaurants, traveled to places around the globe, but now he knew that he'd experienced it all wrong. Money had buffered him from true, honest living. And he'd missed so much—exploring new places, finding rare orchids in the wilderness, and the simple things like catching fish and showering under a waterfall. He would have experienced none of this without her.

Admittedly he could not think of another person on earth he'd rather share these experiences with.

When he looked at her he saw all the things he had not realized he needed. A woman who liked him for who he really was, not the wallet or the image or what prestige they thought they could get from being with him. He wanted to keep Sophia near his heart night and day. But of course, even if he could do that, he would not. Sophia was like a butterfly. She had to be free to shine.

How she'd lit up his world when he'd never even known he was in the dark.

And that expression on her face. It was a come-to-me look if he'd ever seen one.

"Sophia," he said. "I want you so badly I can't breathe."

"I want you, too," she murmured.

"I don't want you to regret this. Are you sure you're just not intoxicated with the joy of finding the ghost orchid?"

"I am intoxicated. With *you*."

"But see, that's the thing. Intoxication wears off and you wake up the next morning hung over and full of apology."

Her eyes met his. "I won't regret this. In fact, if we *don't* make love, that I will regret."

"How can you know for sure?"

"Because passion like this only comes along once in a lifetime. I've been fighting the attraction tooth and nail since you climbed into my plane."

"I know," he said huskily, "so have I."

"But being here." She held her arms wide again. "Among these rare and beautiful flowers, you realize you can't pass up once-in-a-lifetime opportunities when fate presents you with them. I want to grasp the brass ring, Gibb."

"You're absolutely certain?" he rasped.

"I've never been more certain of anything ever."

Gibb couldn't keep his hands off her any longer. He forgot all the reasons why this was not smart and he simply acted. He moved toward her.

Eyes sparkled impishly, and her smile was smug. She stepped toward him, too.

Oh, she knew full well what she did to him.

She toed off her sneakers.

He kicked out of his loafers.

She grabbed hold of the hem of her skimpy little crop top and wrestled it off over her head.

He stopped breathing.

When she dropped her shirt to the ground, giving him a stunning view of her gorgeous breasts filling a pretty pink bra he'd guessed was under there, his heart leaped.

He gulped.

"Are you planning to stand there and stare at me all evening or are you going to unhook my bra?" she whispered in a sleek voice as lovely as the ghost orchids surrounding them. She touched the tip of her tongue to her upper lip and gave him a look that said, *Mister, I'm gonna turn you inside out.*

Part of Gibb wanted to fall to his knees and worship at her beautiful feet, but the alpha male in him rejected the idea and pulled her into his arms.

Thoroughly, ravenously, he kissed her and she kissed him back with the same starving wildness. It had never been like this for him.

Ever.

He wondered if it was special for her, too, or if it was just sex.

She made a low noise and arched, exposing her neck to him. He planted his lips to the sweet spot, while his hands slipped around her to find the clasp of the bra.

"Wait," she said suddenly, pushing him back. "Do you have a condom?"

"In my boxer shorts?"

She gave a high cry of frustration, fisted her hand and pounded lightly on his chest. "In my fantasies, I didn't even think about condoms."

"You've been having fantasies about me?"

"What do you think I've been doing for the past two weeks while I stared at you? Guessing your balance sheet?"

Maybe women before her had, but he was so pleased to hear that she'd been fantasizing about him that he almost panicked because they had no condoms. But then he said, "Sweetheart, there are all kinds of ways we can pleasure each other."

Her smile went sly and she brought up an index finger to stroke his cheek. "Back up."

His mind was so addled it wasn't sure what she was asking of him. "What?"

"Back up against the tree."

He took a step backward, felt the bald cypress at his back, and when he turned his head, he found himself staring at a ghost orchid. "Now what?"

"Hang on. It's going to be a helluva ride." Then she dropped to her knees in front of him, tugging his boxer shorts down around his ankles as she went.

Holy—

He couldn't even finish the thought, he was so aroused and crazy for her. It was completely selfish of him to go first, but he promised in return he'd make her feel so good that she'd always remember him. He'd take his time pleasing her, wanting her to fully experience the moment. Meanwhile, he clenched his hands into fists and closed his eyes.

Her soft fingers took hold of him and his shaft became titanium beneath her touch. All the moisture evaporated from his mouth. Blown. His mind was completely blown.

And she was just getting started.

When the tip of her tongue touched his skin he unraveled. All thoughts flew from his brain and he knew nothing except the feel of her silky mouth on his hot cock.

What an incredible woman she was and how lucky was he. No doubt about either of those two thoughts. He opened his eyes and glanced down at her and his pulse stammered.

Even pressed against the tree, he was knocked off balance. The smell of ghost orchids filled his nose and his knees trembled. Now he knew what the saying "feel the earth move" meant.

She spread her palms over his bare buttocks to steady him, and when she drew him fully into her mouth, Gibb's eyes rolled back in his head. She was licking and stroking and teasing as if she couldn't get enough of him.

He certainly could not get enough of *her*.

Systemically, she dismantled him with her mouth, leaving him breathless and immobile. Someone could have yelled, "Fire!" and he wouldn't have been able to move.

The heat built inside him. Gibb groaned. So good. So damned good.

Her hands slid all over his body. It felt as if she possessed a hundred fingers and ten tongues to do all those amazing things to him.

His chest expanded, tightened. It was unlike anything he'd ever experienced. He touched her head. Such beautiful hair.

"Yes," he hissed, her hair a silky glide beneath his fingers. "Yes, yes, yes."

Sophia worked her magic, with her fingers, and her tongue, leading him somewhere new. He'd been with his share of women, but none had ever made him feel this way. He was consumed. Overtaken. It felt like the most erotic dream in the world.

But this wasn't a dream.

This was really happening.

She was beyond beauty. She was pure life, pure joy. Her mouth moved over him without caution or fear. She pushed him past his knowledge of himself. He had never before been so physically possessed. She rocked his world.

In the haze, Gibb heard the soft beating of moth wings as they suckled at the ghost orchids.

Relentlessly, Sophia sent him beyond the boundaries of his endurance. He was aching, throbbing. He threw back his head and let loose with a primal cry, pleading for release from this magnificent torture, for the ecstasy he could almost touch.

Soon. Please, please let it happen soon. If it didn't, he feared his heart would explode.

He tried to hold back, tried to resist but he could not. She was too damned wonderful.

A bolt of fire rolled along his nerve endings to lodge in the dead center of his throbbing shaft. And then he left the earth, gasping and trembling into the delicious darkness. Lost. He was completely lost. She made it happen.

He blinked, looked down. Finally, he saw her through the haze.

Sophia was sitting at his feet, smiling coyly.

Gibb pitched forward onto his knees and the cushion of soft moss, and then collapsed onto his side. He shuddered, panted for air and tried to wrap his mind around what had just occurred.

Sophia curled up on nature's carpet beside him, rested her head against his back.

In that precious moment, Gibb wanted to change everything about his life and find a whole new way of being.

11

"Your turn," Gibb said after his heart rate slowed and he was breathing normally again. "I've been fantasizing about doing this to you from the minute we left Bosque de Los Dioses."

Too overwhelmed by what she'd done to him, Sophia could not speak. She looked up to find Gibb's eyes on hers. It was clear that he did not think any less of her for her boldness, and in fact, he looked immensely happy.

He rolled her over onto her back on the mossy earth. She went breathless, staring at his washboard abs. Fascinated, Sophia could not look away. He put any athlete to shame.

He was glorious, all biceps and triceps and gluts and hamstrings. She couldn't ever remember having such a well-built lover and she would never forget him.

And his face...

Right now, he was staring at her with those stormy gray eyes that sent goose bumps fleeing up her arm and sweet shivers slivering down her spine.

His jaw was chiseled, his cheekbones sharp, his

sandy hair cut in a short, no-nonsense style—all business, this one—nothing frivolous about him.

The setting was magical. Ghost orchids bloomed around them, filling the air with their rich scent. The golden sun had disappeared. Time stretched out before them, languid and endless. She forgot all about getting off the island. Why would she ever want to leave paradise?

He lowered his head and kissed her slowly, gently. She closed her eyes, inhaled him, savored each delicious taste. A minute later, he pulled back and smiled down at her so tender, so genuine, that emotion blocked her throat.

"Gibb," she said. "We have to talk."

"Yes, I need to know everything. Likes, dislikes, how much pressure, how—"

She put an index finger to his lips. "Shh."

He said nothing, just stared deeply into her eyes.

"Listen." Sophia paused, not sure how to phrase what she had to say.

"All ears, Amelia."

She couldn't help smiling. There was just something about him that made her want to smile all the time. "We need to set up some ground rules here."

"I might have given the impression I'm a sophisticated guy," he said, "but when it comes to sex, the basics work for me. I don't need anything kinky." He wriggled his eyebrows. "That is unless there's something you want to try."

"I'm not talking about those kinds of ground rules," she said.

He cocked his head. "I'm not really following you."

She made a little X over his heart. "I'm talking about emotional ground rules."

"Oh." His eyes clouded. "Those ground rules."

Sophia gathered her courage. She liked Gibb, probably more than she had any right to like him, but this had to be said. If they didn't get this straight right up front, she was so afraid she would get lost in the passion. She'd spent her life waiting for this ground-shaking feeling and now that it was here, she was terrified of where it might—or might not—lead. That was the scary part, the not knowing where she stood.

"I'm listening," he prompted.

"We don't know what will happen once we go back to our regular lives."

"What do you want to have happen?"

Happily-ever-after cried her heart, but she was too timid to say that. They hardly knew each other, although forced proximity had accelerated their relationship. They were so different. They came from completely different worlds. Was passion enough? For the first time, she understood what Josie had been trying to tell her when she said there were other things of value in a loving relationship beyond passion.

"I don't want to get hurt," she whispered.

A look that she couldn't read passed over his eyes. He nodded. "I understand. I want to keep things light, too. We can do that. You're right. Good idea to set ground rules. We can relieve some tension and enjoy our time together."

"Yes," she said, even though she wanted him to say, "Forget it, let's jump headfirst into this thing." She knew that was utterly unrealistic. If she was smart, she'd call a stop to this right now, but she wanted him so much.

Pathetic.

Still, wasn't one night of intense passion better than nothing at all?

"I just didn't want you to confuse fun for something else," she said in a scratchy voice.

"No worries. I'm a big boy."

"That's good."

"Okay." He dropped his lips to her throat. "Now where were we? Oh, yes, let's get you out of those clothes."

She'd never been particularly modest, but suddenly, she felt shy as his fingers slipped around her back to unhook her bra.

Her breasts bounced free.

Gibb was eyeing them lustily, the heat of his gaze caused her nipples to pucker.

Embarrassed, she crossed her arms over her chest. "My brothers used to call me *Tortita*."

"What does that mean?"

"Pancake."

He laughed.

She pretended to be affronted. "You don't have to agree with them."

"On the contrary, I disagree with them heartily." He lowered his eyelashes and murmured, "Perfect."

Overwhelmed by the hungry look on his face, she closed her eyes.

He cupped her face in both his hands and then he stopped. She wanted to open her eyes, to see what was going on, but she didn't want to meet his gaze. Too worried about the emotion she might spot in his eyes.

She could feel his breath on her cheeks. He said nothing. Neither did she. A minute ticked by. Sounds of the jungle at night heightened the tension.

Do something! Kiss me. Touch me. Anything.

Finally, she could stand the suspense no longer and cautiously opened one eye.

Gibb was looking at her as if she were a precious treasure he'd found on the beach. His lips landed on hers, a searing brand.

She sighed, threaded her fingers through his hair.

He stroked her chin and the gesture was so tender Sophia felt the urge to burst into tears. Hormones, she told herself. That's all it was. She could not afford to love this guy. They had no future together.

Because no matter how much Gibb wanted her sexually, he really didn't want her for happily ever after. She knew this, even if he did not. She was too content for a goal-driven man like him. He needed someone as rich as he was, someone who understood how to navigate his world.

That most decidedly was not her. She might be half American by birth, but she was pure Costa Rican by nature. She loved her life. Wanted for nothing.

Except for passionate love.

Which she had right this minute. So what if it couldn't last?

She thought he was quivering, and then realized that it was she, shaking so hard the thick, humid air seemed to ripple.

He burned hot kisses from her throat to her breasts, his beard stubble rubbing her skin in a wholly erotic rasp. He was smooth and accomplished, no doubt about it. He knew exactly where to linger, tease and cajole. His hand went to the snap of her denim shorts.

She whimpered his name.

He slid the zipper down.

She stopped breathing.

"Raise your hips," he instructed.

She obeyed.

He slipped her shorts and underwear off of her in one smooth motion, leaving her exposed and trembling.

"Mmm," he growled low in his throat. "You smell so good."

He began a slow slide from the tender flesh of her breasts on down to where she most wanted him to go. He trailed silent kisses over her rib cage to her taut, flat belly, and then veered down to lick the warm, damp patch of skin between her legs.

Sophia came unglued.

"Ah," he said. "You like that."

"Yes," she gasped.

He paused there, driving her mad with need. Her muscles tensed and then every nerve ending in her body started tingling as she tried to anticipate his next move.

Gibb surprised her by reaching up to skim his fingers over her face, outlining the plane of her cheeks with the pads of his fingertips like a blind man learning Braille. With incredible lightness, he stroked the base of his palm over her collarbone.

"Sophia," he breathed.

She smiled.

His hand trailed back to the triangle of hair and he stared deeply into her eyes. She was so ready for him.

"Please," she said softly.

Slowly, he stroked and teased her, and she rode the

flow of emotions, embracing the swell of pleasure and desire and discovery. His warmth enveloped her and she experienced a sense of safety with him that she'd rarely felt before. He lifted her to a place she'd never known existed.

She moaned and pushed her pelvis against his hand, arching her back in the soft jungle carpet. She drifted on the edge of a dark peak, engulfed by the feel of him, the dampness of the night, the smell of ghost orchids, the music of his breathing and the sight of his gorgeous, muscular body. Sophia wanted him too much. The passion was consuming her. She'd slipped too far.

A bittersweet thought seized her. As wonderful as this moment was, it could not last. She closed her eyes, determined to ignore the sadness. Besides, this was all she needed, this brief slice of delight.

He cradled his head against her thigh. He ran one hand down and then up the opposite leg, before tickling higher on the returning stroke.

"Your touch," she whispered. "Unbelievable."

She shuddered as his lips skipped over the last firm curve of her thigh, stopping just short of her core. Her body was on fire for him.

Gibb moved his head closer, slightly touching his lips to her intimate folds. He showered her there with rich, tender kisses.

Her senses swam with each movement he made.

He curved his palm over her soft mound and, reaching the spot where her skin began to part, he stroked her gently. His hot mouth found her willing center. She curled her fingers into her palms, cried out in the darkness.

His tongue did wicked, wicked things that sent her

pulse spiking and just when he had her writhing and breathless, he retreated.

"No, no," she said. "Don't you dare tease me!"

He laughed.

She reached down and gripped his shoulders for support.

"You taste so good," he murmured and went back to what he was doing and she exhaled a big sigh. He put his tongue to her most sensitive spot and it was like switching on a light in a darkened room.

"Yes, yes," she cried. "You know exactly where and how to touch me. How do you know that?"

"You're very responsive," he said. "Your body tells me what to do."

He kissed and caressed her, cupping his hands around her buttocks to lift her higher. His warm breath sent a humming sensation vibrating up through her body.

Automatically, she arched against his mouth. "Don't stop, don't stop," she chanted.

Gibb kept it up, giving her everything she craved.

Moaning loudly, she tensed, feeling the sweet pressure building inside her. His tongue obliterated everything. She could do nothing except focus on that one sensitive spot.

Unbearable. How sweet his seductive torture was. She thrashed against him.

Gradually, he released her, but kept his tongue playing across her soft skin. He toyed with her until she cried out his name over and over. He owned every inch of her body. She was his, in the palm of his hand. She would do anything he asked.

She made a strangled noise. Close. She was so very close.

"Hold on, baby. The wait will be worth it," he promised.

And then it happened, uncontrollable spasms gripped her body and she shattered against the most amazing mouth in the whole wide world.

SOPHIA WAS NAKED, bristling with sexuality, her veins fire and fervor, muscles melted soft, tendons stretched loose, body sore and liquid.

Who knew a man could do such incredible things with a tongue? Gibb had fallen asleep beside her, his legs intertwined with hers. She curled her toes and smiled into the darkness.

She and Gibb were as much a part of nature as the night birds and creatures prowling the underbrush. She let out a long, slow breath, felt her body relax. Many people would be terrified not knowing what lurked in the shadows, but Sophia had been raised in a tropical forest. The sounds and smells were as comforting to her as a lullaby.

Home.

The rustling did not scare her. No, what really concerned her was the man beside her. Gibb was from a completely different kind of jungle. One that was not as easy to predict as hers.

She turned her head, flipping her hair up from behind her back where it pulled and basked in his body heat. Nothing could have prepared her for the depth of emotions tightening her stomach. It had been so easy to get caught up in the vortex of their attraction, but once ensnared, how hard was it going to be to get out of this unscathed?

Sex was just sex. Right?

That's what people tried to tell you and maybe sometimes it was, but when you had this kind of chemistry with another person…well…it was as if her heart had split open wide and the sun was pouring both into her and out of her, bathing everything in an impossibly bright light.

She closed her eyes, swallowed past the lump in her throat. It was too bad she hadn't felt anything like this for Emilio. He was a good man, a great friend and probably even a competent lover.

Or so she'd assumed, until Gibb.

Now, nothing or no one could ever compare to him.

Terrifying, that what she'd just experienced was the pinnacle of her love life. After Gibb, every other man would pale in comparison.

She reached up to touch Gibb's face in the darkness. Traced his nose with her index finger, such a masculine nose, straight and commanding. He was so vibrant, so virile. Why couldn't he have been a normal man with a normal job? Not a billionaire so far out of her reach it was laughable.

That was enough regret. She had to change her thinking. Even though this had been the hottest sexual encounter of her life, she could not romanticize it. No more imagining far-flung places, no more dreaming about what it would be like to wake beside him every morning. Most likely it wouldn't be all that great anyway. He was a workaholic. No doubt he was up before dawn, spent an hour at the gym before a limo picked him up to whisk him off for a sixteen-hour day at the office.

Eventually, her memory of this romantic rendezvous would fade and every once in a while, whenever she saw something that reminded her of him—El Diablo for instance or spider monkeys or passion fruit—she'd smile slyly and leave everyone guessing why.

Until Gibb, she had believed she would never settle for anything in a relationship except fiery passion. Now she knew firsthand that passion was a double-edged sword that cut both ways. While passion was the most intoxicating thing, it robbed you of your reasoning, dazzled your body and dazed your mind.

With this kind of passion, how did anyone ever get anything done? She and Gibb would be in bed ninety-nine percent of the time. He'd lose his billions. She'd never fly again.

Ah, but she would fly in a wholly different way.

She bit her bottom lip. Floated in the drunken embrace of lovemaking's afterglow. What would it be like with him all the time?

That was just the thing, wasn't it? Maybe this was fair warning. A danger signal. Ease off. Don't go any further. Stop now and turn back before it's too late.

But if switching off her need for him was that easy, she wouldn't be here right now, basking in this bliss. She shivered, remembering the feel of his lips on her skin.

Gibb moved, reached out, and tugged her closer. He pressed a kiss to her forehead.

"Gibb?"

"Hmm?"

"Are you awake?"

"No."

"That was…you were…I mean…well, I'm speechless."

"Me, too, sweetheart," he murmured.

She buried her face against his neck, inhaled his scent. She felt as if she were walking barefoot across a high line wire. One slip and she'd be electrified.

Who was she kidding? She was gone already.

She could hear the hammering of his heart. Her heart was hammering, too.

Shouldn't she get up? Put some distance between them so she could think this thing through? Ah, but it was so easy to rest against him, so easy to allow herself to get swept away. Not smart. Not smart at all, but she'd been raised to do what she loved. That if she lived with heart and passion that she would be wealthy in the ways that counted.

Unexpected tears rose to her eyes and her nose burned. She pressed her lips together. No. Nothing to cry about. This was beautiful and she would enjoy every last second of it and when it was gone, well, she prayed she'd be strong enough to let go.

Slowly, she drifted off to sleep.

She was having an erotic dream. She and Gibb were doing all kinds of interesting things to each other with food—smearing chocolate syrup over their bodies and licking it off, eating strawberry Pop Rocks and kissing, feeding each other from clusters of ripe red grapes. So immersed was she in the dream, that at first she thought the faraway buzzing sound was part of the dream. That maybe Gibb had found a beehive and he was raiding it for honey to use in their sex play.

It took a few minutes for the noise to fully seep into her consciousness. Airplane. Not bees at all. It was the sound of an airplane engine.

Sophia blinked awake, cocked her head to listen. Was it really an airplane or just her dream?

The familiar droning lit her up inside. No dream. It *was* a plane.

She flung Gibb's arm off her chest. Jumped to her feet. The darkness of the jungle was slipping away. Dawn was approaching.

"What is it? What's wrong?" Gibb asked groggily. He sat up, rubbed his eyes.

Even in her haste, Sophia could not stop herself from casting a glance over his naked body. Hombre sexy.

"Soph?"

She pointed toward the sky. "Plane."

Instantly he was on his feet. "The radio. We have to get to the radio."

"Clothes. Shoes."

"On it."

She searched the dark ground and her fingers hit material. Silk. She thrust his boxer shorts at him. He handed Sophia her cotton crop top.

"Hurry, hurry."

"We'll never make it to the beach in time," he muttered.

"Don't think negatively."

"Do you know the way out of here?"

"I think I do. I heard the ocean waves during the night. I don't think we're all that far from the beach."

"But what if where we come out is on the opposite side of the island from the plane?"

"We have to try."

"You're daydreaming."

"Exactly. Remember where daydreaming got me," she reminded him.

They found their shoes and put them on.

The airplane noises were growing fainter. Still, the plane would be in radio range even when they could no longer hear the engine. It all depended on how long it took them to get to the beach.

"Come on," she cried, and grabbed Gibb's hand.

_12_

STUMBLING OVER ROOTS and vines, they ran toward where she thought the beach might be, following the lulling sound of the ocean. All around them animals and insects scurried out of their way.

After several minutes, Sophia was out of breath, but Gibb was an iron man, taking the lead and battling back the vegetation so she could follow him unimpeded. Who knew the city man was in better physical condition than a woman who'd grown up walking mountains? He was something else. Even in haste, she couldn't help appreciating his body. The man had a lot to be proud of.

She was beginning to despair that they wouldn't make it to the beach in time. The sound of the airplane engine was long gone, but there was still hope. Since the plane had been flying at an altitude low enough for them to hear it, there was a possibility that the pilot spotted El Diablo on the beach. Wishful thinking, yes, but then again, maybe it was a rescue plane.

A man like Gibb Martin did not go missing without people noticing, but it had still been dark when she'd first heard the engine. Had it been too dark for the pilot to see her plane?

While she and Gibb had been out having frantic sex, they might have lost their opportunity to be rescued for several days. Why, then, was she not upset by the prospect of spending more time on the island alone with Gibb?

Um, remember, you don't have any condoms.

Stranded on a deserted island with the sexiest man alive. A man she had dynamite chemistry with and no condoms. It was her definition of torture.

At last, she could see the faint glow of dawn filtering through the trees as the vegetation grew sparser. They were almost to the frustration.

Gibb broke through the last column of fronds. He paused, looked back and waited for her.

"Go, go." Panting, she waved at him. "Get to the radio."

"No," he said and held out his palm. "We're in this together."

Touched, she slipped her hand into his.

He gripped her tight. "We're a team."

They stepped over a fallen log, skirted a clump of felled coconuts and their feet hit sand.

El Diablo sat at least five hundred yards away.

She groaned. More running.

"You can do it," Gibb encouraged. "I have complete faith in you."

"Easy for you to say. Your legs are much longer than mine. I have to take two steps for every one of yours."

From the ocean on the other side of El Diablo a small boat bobbed in the water.

"Hey, look." Gibb grinned at her. "We can slow down. Someone's here to save us."

Sophia squinted into the pale sunlight and an uneasy feeling spread over her. That second sense she seemed to have about people, was warning her. She stopped.

Gibb took a few more steps before he realized she was not keeping up with him. He halted, turned back.

Instinct told her to step back into the tree line.

"Sophia?" he said. "What is it?"

She put an index finger to her lips, shook her head.

"What's wrong?" he whispered.

She kept walking backward, step-by-step and crooked her index finger at him.

"Soph?" He frowned, looked from her to the boat and back again.

For a moment, she thought that he was not going to follow her and she would have to say something. Although the people in the boat probably weren't close enough to hear them, she didn't want to take any chances.

This island most likely belonged to Columbia like the nearby Island de Providencia. Maybe they were drug smugglers who hid their cache of drugs on the island. A ripple of fear moved through her and she kept walking until she was hidden from view.

Gibb came after her. "Sophia, what's going on?"

"Shh." She crouched down, hid behind a banana tree and peeked around the wide leaves.

The boat was getting closer. There were three men in it.

Gibb crouched beside her. "You want to clue me in about what's happening here?"

"I don't know."

"Hmm, so you don't know why we're hiding out from our rescuers?"

"We don't know that they *are* here to rescue us. Better to err on the side of caution."

"If they're not here to rescue us, who do you think they are?"

She shrugged. "Pirates. Drug smugglers. Who knows? This island is remote and we have nothing to defend ourselves with."

"We could lob coconuts at them, or hey, passion fruit. They really stung when the monkeys pelted us with them."

She glowered at him.

"You're serious about this?"

"Yes."

"Wow." Both eyebrows shot up on his forehead.

"We are alone. We do not know who these men are. We have no way of communicating with the outside world."

"Don't you think you're being a bit paranoid?" he said. "What if they came here to look for us and we're so busy hiding that they leave and no one comes by for a good long time?"

What if that did happen? Sophia bit her bottom lip. What if her instincts were wrong?

Gibb said nothing for a few minutes. They crouched together as the boat grew nearer and nearer. It was going to come ashore right where El Diablo was grounded.

"Look, I understand why you're nervous. You're a woman. It's important not to be too trusting around men you don't know, but after last night, I figured you'd trust me to take care of you."

"It's not that I don't trust you," she said. "I just have a bad feeling about this."

"Any particular reason why?"

"The boat is old and looks to be in poor condition. Would rescuers arrive in such a boat?"

"You make a good point."

The boat was close enough now that they could hear the men speaking. She couldn't make out the words but it was clear they were speaking Spanish.

Gibb scooted closer to her. "Can you hear what they're saying?"

"They're still too far away."

"Sophia, I respect your intuition, but I can't simply hide here and let the opportunity to be rescued pass us by. If we get out of here today, I can still make it to Florida before Scott's wedding."

"Will you let that go already?"

"I can't," he said. "You were right before when you said that I focus more on goals than relationships. Scott is important to me. It's time for me to put friendship ahead of money."

"So what is your plan? Just walk right out there and say, *'Hola'*? You don't even speak Spanish."

"Let's say they aren't here to rescue us. Just some fishermen who saw the plane and curiosity got the better of them. I'm certain that I could convince them to take us to Island de Providencia for the right price. I do know the Spanish word for money."

"I bet you know the word 'money' in a hundred languages." She flipped her hair back over her shoulder.

"It's a plan. You wanted to know my plan. That's it."

"Pirates do not take credit cards. And since you are an American, they will assume you are rich. Those expensive silk boxer shorts would cement the impression. They'll take you hostage and I don't even want to think about what they might do to me."

That got through to him. He curled his hand around her shoulder. "You really are serious."

"Let's just wait and listen to their conversation when they come ashore. If it's about fishing and concern that someone's plane crashed, then we'll come out of hiding."

"All right," he agreed.

She had convinced him, but now Sophia had to wonder if maybe she was being too suspicious. Could this feeling be a subconscious desire to spend more time alone with Gibb, rather than a real sixth sense about the men in the boat?

The boat landed on the beach.

The hairs on the back of Sophia's neck stood up. Something was definitely not right here.

The men climbed out of the boat and walked over to El Diablo. One of the men picked up Gibb's suit pants from where she'd left the garment drying on the wing of the plane. He spoke to his companions. They laughed.

"What did he say?" Gibb asked.

"The pilot must be a naked rich man," she translated.

"Naked is a bit of an overstatement."

She flicked a glance at his butt in those silk boxer shorts. "Not by much."

"And what's with the assumption that I'm rich?"

"Thieves are pretty good at spotting expensive things. There are times when a fancy suit is a drawback. Wear shorts once in a while, why don't you?"

"So they do know we're here," he said inanely.

"The crashed plane was pretty self-evident."

The other two men motioned for the first to come back to the boat. The man tossed Gibb's pants over the wing.

Gibb stood up. "They're leaving."

"No, they're not."

The men removed a large blue plastic tub from the boat.

Gibb squatted down again. "What do you suppose they have in that thing?"

"Drugs. Pirate treasure. A body. Who knows?"

"For a happy woman you can go to some pretty dark places."

She made a pipe-down motion. "They're talking."

The man that had found Gibb's pants pulled a piece of paper from his back pocket and unfolded it. A map.

"Maybe they're lost," Gibb said.

"Shh."

The tallest of the men made another trip to the boat and returned with two digging spades. That looked ominous. They were speaking low and she could only catch snatches of Spanish words—harvest, shears, potting soil.

Gibb nudged her with his elbow. "What are they talking about?"

Sophia crinkled her nose. "Gardening supplies."

"They're gardeners?"

She shook her head just as the tallest man again reached into the boat. The man with the map thumped it with his hand and said, *"Fantasma,"* at the same time the tallest man retrieved what he'd gone after, slung it over his shoulder.

"Do you know who they are?" Gibb asked.

"I do. They're orchid thieves and they've got a gun."

SOPHIA'S INTUITION HAD been right. The men were up to no good and the appearance of a shotgun was disturbing. However, this could work to their advantage if they were careful. Stay hidden here until the men disappeared into the jungle after the orchids, then he and Sophia could steal their boat and motor off to Island de Providencia.

Before Gibb had a chance to voice his plan, Sophia grabbed his elbow and pulled him deeper into the tropical forest.

"Where are we going?"

"To save the ghost orchids."

He balked, dug his heels in. "I hate to point out the obvious, but shouldn't we be waiting until they go into the jungle and then we take off in their boat?"

She stared at him like he had suggested she kick a kitten. "We can't let them steal the orchids."

"Sure we can. It will keep them occupied while we get away."

"You don't get it. These are ghost orchids. The rarest orchids in the world."

"I agree, it's sad for beautiful wild orchids to fall into the hands of smugglers, but they do have a shotgun and I don't want to end up on the wrong end of—"

Sophia wasn't listening. She turned and moved along the way they'd come.

Ah, hell, he was going to have to follow her. There was one drawback to a passionate woman. When she set her mind on something, it was set.

"Wait," he called as loud as he dared. The worst thing that they could do would be to get separated.

She waited for him to catch up to her. "We'll have to be quick," she whispered.

He had no idea what she was thinking of, but at this point, he simply took it on faith. She had been right about the men in the boat. That shotgun made him a firm believer in her female intuition.

It took him and Sophia fifteen minutes to find their way back to the orchids.

"We don't have much time." She pulled the Swiss Army knife from her pocket and started hacking viciously at vines. "Gather them up as I cut them."

He was totally confused. "What are we doing?"

"Last ditch effort to save the orchids." She was a jungle ninja, running and cutting vines.

Stunned, he started gathering the downed vines, measuring roughly six to eight feet in length. What she was doing made no sense, but he trusted her.

By the time she finished slashing, she was panting and her cheeks were flushed. She cut at least a dozen vines.

"Tie a slipknot by folding the vine in two sections. One side should be several feet long, the second side only a few inches, like this." She demonstrated as she talked. "Now pull the folded end of the vine up several inches so that you form three loops like this."

"I'll do it, sure, but can you tell me what we're making?"

"Snare nooses."

"You mean like trappers once used to catch wild animals?"

"Exactly. Pay attention. String the right loop and pull it tight, but make sure to keep a noose in the end. The end of the knot should be large enough to slip the vine through. Finally, slide the long end of the vine through the knot."

He was highly skeptical that this crazy plan would work, but he indulged her. They could always go back to his plan while the smugglers were busy digging up orchids. The one thing that bothered him though was the shotgun.

"How's this?" he asked, holding up the snare noose he'd made.

"Looks good. That's two. Keep going. The more we have the more likely we are to catch them."

"You plan on catching these men with vines?"

"My brothers caught me in a snare noose more than once."

"Really?" He was impressed.

"But I was a kid and didn't weigh much. Like I said, this is a last ditch effort to save the ghost orchids."

"Is there really that much of a market for illegal orchids?"

"One ghost orchid plant alone would be worth thousands. The tragedy is, I seriously doubt these men are accomplished horticulturists and orchids are delicate. They'll steal them all in the hopes that one or two plants will make it."

"How do you know so much about orchids?"

"Orchids were the reason my American mother came to Costa Rica. They were her greatest passion until she met my father." Sophia tied three snare nooses before he finished his second.

"She sounds like quite a woman, your mother. Must be where you get your spunk."

She flashed him a tense smile. "Thank you."

"For what?"

"Granting me this chance. I know saving an endangered flower is probably not a big deal to you…"

He looked her squarely in the eye. "Sophia, I appreciate rare and beautiful things."

Her lips parted and her eyes flared warm and grateful. Had she understood he was talking about her?

She cast a glance over her shoulder. "Let us listen and see if we can hear them coming."

They worked in silence until they'd made a dozen nooses. They heard noises in the forest, but no human footsteps. Not yet.

"What now?" Gibb asked.

"We set the snares." She showed him how to set the traps. They had six hidden and set on the jungle floor when they heard the men's voices.

"They're coming," he said. "We have to leave. I'm not going to risk them finding you."

"The more snares we get—"

"Sophia," he said firmly, brooking no argument and taking hold of her arm. "Let's go. Now."

THEY HID AMONG the vegetation on the opposite side of the clearing from where they'd set the traps.

Sophia rubbed her sweaty palms against her shorts. Humidity plastered her hair to her head. This had to work. If it didn't work the beautiful orchids would be destroyed. It was probably illogical, this determination to try to save the orchids. Gibb's plan had been much more rational. Steal the smugglers' boat while they were stealing the orchids and get away to safety. But that would mean leaving both the orchids and El Diablo vulnerable and she couldn't do that without making a last ditch effort to stop the thieves.

Her knees were starting to ache from crouching.

Where were those orchid thieves? They had a map. What was taking them so long?

Gibb rested a hand on her shoulder and immediately she was soothed. "Patience."

She shifted her position to kneel on the ground. Her heartbeat throbbed loudly in her ears. The smell of ghost orchids filled the air. Gibb had looked straight at her when he said he appreciated rare and beautiful things. Well, in her eyes, he was the rare and beautiful thing, as rare and beautiful as a ghost orchid, whereas she was as common as a weed.

It was comforting to have him with her. They did make a great team and she was surprised at how easily he'd picked up fashioning noose snares. Gibb Martin was a quick study and she was lucky to have known him.

She wrapped her arms around herself as sadness wrapped her in its damp arms. Soon, this adventure would be over and she and Gibb would return to their own lives and be nothing more to each other than a sweet memory of a short, red-hot affair. *Don't think about it now. Orchid thieves are coming. Be on guard.*

Male voices and the sound of heavy footsteps could be heard. The men were not far away.

"¿Qué crees que sucedió a la gente en el avión?"

Gibb squeezed her arm.

Sophia pressed her lips to his ear, breathed in his masculine scent and whispered, "They're wondering where we are. If they catch us…"

He slipped his arm around her waist, held her against him, and gave her a look that said *I would die before I let them hurt you.*

In front of them, the vegetation parted and the first

man appeared. It was the one who had found Gibb's suit and he was carrying the shotgun.

Ice froze Sophia's blood.

The man took one look at the orchids, and his eyes widened. *"Ah, la orquidea fantasma!"* he exclaimed.

The other two men appeared carrying the blue plastic tub and the garden spades. They dropped their load and stood staring with their mouths hanging open.

The ghosts were a spectacular sight, but Sophia knew the men were seeing the flowers not for their rare beauty, but for the many dollars they would bring.

The first man settled the shotgun down on top of the blue plastic tub.

Sophia tasted hope. Maybe, just maybe, this loco idea of hers would work. Beside her, Gibb tensed, ready to spring into action.

The three men rushed forward at once, but time seemed to slow curiously. Sophia held her breath.

The first man hit a noose snare seconds before the others. The trap snagged his ankle, and the long end of the vine jerked him upward into the bald cypress where Gibb had secured the other end. Blindsided, the man screamed out.

His buddies whipped around, distress on their faces. The second man stepped backward into another snare noose and he too was flung upward. The two men dangled upside down, blinking and looking confused.

The third man sprang for the shotgun.

This was what Sophia had dreaded, that not all the snares would work and one or more of the men would get away.

Gibb leaped to his feet, charged through the clearing like an enraged bull elephant, letting loose with a frightening war cry.

Caught off guard, Sophia fell backward onto her butt.

The third man grabbed up the gun, pivoted. He was going to shoot Gibb! If Gibb got shot it would be all her fault.

"No!" Sophia screamed.

But Gibb was quicker. Head down, he rammed the man in the kidneys like a linebacker sacking a quarterback. The shotgun flew from the man's hands.

Sophia didn't even remember how she'd got there. Raw instinct and emotion must have driven her. One minute she was there on the ground, the next minute she had the shotgun in her hands, and she was standing over the orchid thief, the barrel pressed flat against his belly, one eye closed as she stared down the site.

With a cocky flourish, she threatened, *"No se mueven."* Don't move.

13

GIBB CHUCKLED ALL the way back to the plane as they marched the three wannabe orchid smugglers ahead of them. Again and again, he pictured that priceless moment when Sophia jammed the gun into the thief's belly and spouted that classic line, her long dark hair swirling around her, her eyes narrowed, her face intense.

She was the coolest woman in the world. What a badass, his little Sophia!

They'd found duct tape amid the orchid harvesting supplies and made good use of it by binding the sullen men's hands behind their backs. They were none too pleased to have been bested by a woman.

That made Gibb chuckle even more. Don't mess with the daughter of an orchid-loving mother.

When they arrived at the beach, Gibb made the men get into the boat. Keeping the shotgun pointed at them just in case they got some silly idea about trying to escape, he stepped over to the plane where Sophia was rummaging for her tool kit.

"You were impressively awesome back there," he told her.

"Not so bad yourself. Head butting the guy."

"See, proof that we make a good team."

Her eyes sparkled.

"Sophia…" He paused, not sure what he wanted to say.

She took his platinum bracelet from her pocket. "Are you ready for this?"

Was he? Sure, he wanted to get off the island, but once they were on their way, everything would change. This had been a special moment in time and he didn't want it to end, but it wasn't reality. They both knew that.

He gulped. Nodded.

"I'll have to destroy the bracelet. You do understand that."

"Yes."

"Just making sure because I know it's a symbol of your bond with your buddy."

"I appreciate that."

She stared deeply into his eyes. "We don't have to do it, you know? Now that we have the boat."

His chest tightened. "It would take us much longer to get to Island de Providencia by boat and we would be abandoning your plane."

"I see." She looked disappointed, as if she *wanted* to take longer to get to civilization. Or maybe it was wishful thinking on his part.

"See what?"

"You're still determined to break up your friend's impending marriage."

"Yeah," he said, because he didn't know what else to say. "I guess I am."

She shook her head.

"What?"

"It all comes down to what you're willing to sacrifice, doesn't it?"

Gibb frowned. "What do you mean?"

"Give up the symbol of your brotherhood with Scott." She dangled the bracelet from her fingers. "Or give up control."

The scar on his chest twinged. He pressed his knuckles against it. Was she right? Was this all a bid for control on his part?

"Symbol loses," she said and took a pair of wire cutters from her tool kit and handed them to him. "You do the honors."

After glancing over at the men in the boat who glowered at him, he set down the shotgun. Gibb gripped the handle of the cutters, slipped the short, sharp blade between the links. Images flashed through his mind of that trip to the Great Barrier Reef. The stingray attack. The pain. Scott's face blurring as Gibb slipped in and out of consciousness. Then later, when they got their matching bracelets and strapped them on their wrists simultaneously.

To severe the bond or not?

Preserve the bracelet, but by doing so miss the opportunity to stop Scott from making a grave mistake. Or snap the link and hopefully achieve his goal.

His eyes met Sophia's. She waited patiently. "Are you pretty sure this will work?"

"I think so, but there's no guarantee."

You had to take a big risk to gain big, right? Just do it. Just make a decision and act. That had always been the secret of his success. Why was he waffling now?

Resolutely, Gibb clipped the bracelet.

IN LESS THAN an hour, Sophia repaired the rudder cable and they took off from the island. Gibb was back in his suit, although it was a little worse for wear.

They gave the men in the boat water before they left them. When they arrived in Island de Providencia they would send the authorities to apprehend the thieves.

The takeoff was smooth, professional, the rudder patch job made with links from his platinum bracelet worked. But of course, Sophia was both an accomplished pilot and mechanic.

During the short flight, they spoke of nothing important—the clean shower they wanted to take, the good meal they hoped to eat. Sophia mused about getting a new cable put on her rudder. Gibb tried to keep from being obvious when he sneaked glances over at her. God, the woman was stunning in so many ways. Neither one of them spoke about the sexy night they'd spent in the jungle. Already, it seemed so far away.

They landed on Island de Providencia a little after one o'clock on Friday afternoon. Had it really been less than forty-eight hours since they'd left Bosque de Los Dioses? It seemed a lifetime ago.

Sophia headed for the FBO to see if they had a mechanic on duty who might be willing to replace the cable. Before she left, he slipped her a credit card. "To grease the wheels."

She started to protest, but he balked. "Your plane broke because of me and I said I would cover all expenses. Take it."

"Thank you."

"Thank *you*."

They lingered for a moment, and then she turned and walked inside the building, leaving Gibb with a choice to make. When should he have his private jet come pick him up? At this point, he couldn't worry about whether spies were tracking his plane or not. Getting a commercial flight out of here would be a logistical nightmare.

The issue was how close did he want to cut it?

He used a cell phone app to calculate the time and distance from Miami, where his corporate jet was hangered, to Island de Providencia. The flight would take four to five hours. He could be in Key West before midnight if he asked his pilot to leave now.

Or…

Just then, Sophia came out of the FBO smiling and waving his credit card.

Or, he could have his pilot pick him up early tomorrow morning and have one last night with Sophia. His heart knocked at the thought.

He pocketed his phone and moved toward her.

Note to self. Buy plenty of condoms.

She hurried over to him.

"Hi." Gibb smiled back, feeling sappy and romantic.

"Hi," Sophia answered breathlessly.

"Did you find someone to replace the cable?"

"It seems to be my lucky day. They have a cable that fits my plane and they can install it this afternoon. The credit card you gave me to grease the wheels went a long way. Thank you."

"I was thinking," he said, "since we're both waiting on transportation, after we report the orchid thieves to the police, that maybe we could get a motel room, have a shower, buy some clean clothes, grab a bite to eat…"

"Make love?" she dared.

He lowered his eyelids. "That, too."

She surprised him by leaning in to plant a quick kiss on his lips. "I thought you'd never ask."

By 7:00 P.M. that evening they were sitting on the patio of a beachside bungalow drinking rum cocktails with little pink umbrellas in them. Sophia wore a red spaghetti-strap sundress that Gibb had bought at an overpriced tourist boutique and he had on khaki shorts and a blue V-neck T-shirt. They were enjoying the sunset and eating sweet-flesh langostino with their fingers.

She gave him the once over. "I like seeing you this way. Relaxed, unhurried, loose."

"I have to admit, I like being this way. It's nice. Being here with you is nice."

"Ditto."

They sighed in contented unison. Too bad it couldn't last forever.

"Mmm," Sophia said, popping the last langostino into her mouth and licking her fingers. "Beats the heck out of wieners."

"I don't know about that. I really enjoyed our campfire cookout." Playfully, he reached out to run his foot along the back of her calf.

"You know what I keep thinking about?" she murmured.

"What's that?"

"The box of condoms you bought."

Gibb's grin stretched from one side of his face to the other. "Say the word, sweetheart, and I'm there."

She got to her feet, held her hand out to him. "Word."

He guided her into the bungalow and they fell into bed like it was the most natural thing ever. There was no awkwardness between them. Everything flowed like

they were a couple who had been dancing the tango together every day for fifty years.

Gibb undressed her slowly. Kissing her between each
step. Down her arm went one spaghetti strap and he
gave her three kisses, one on the lips, and two on the
neck.

He went on like this for the longest, loveliest time
and then he stopped, took her chin in his hand and tilted
her face up to him. "Should we talk about this?"

She shrugged. "What is there to say?"

"I thought after everything that has happened we
might want to explore the possibility—"

She shook her head. "There is no need to define what
we are doing. No need to give it a name. Just be in the
moment, Gibb. Enjoy what is in front of us."

"Are you sure this is what you want?"

"We have tonight. It's enough. Tomorrow you will
fly east and I will fly west. We will go our separate
ways."

"We'll see each other again. When I return to Bosque
de Los Dioses."

"We should not continue our relationship after tonight. What we had on that island, what we're about to
have on this island, won't hold up in the light of day.
The flame will burn out in the clash of our real worlds.
In your heart you know that." She splayed a palm over
his scarred chest. "There is nothing wrong with seizing
the moment and sucking every last ounce of pleasure
from it and then letting go."

His eyes glittered in the dim light. "Is that what you
really want?"

"Yes," she lied.

She did not want him to say something that would

give her hope, because she knew they were a mismatched pair. Soon enough, he would go back to his hectic world and come to see that the time he'd spent with her was nothing but a lovely interlude. She was okay with that. Just as long as she didn't have hope that they could be anything more than they already were—temporary lovers.

They looked at each other and the fire rolled over them. The passion they felt for each other could no longer be denied. They finished stripping off their clothes in a mad frenzy, foreplay be damned.

Her bare belly was pressed against his flat, rippled abdomen and his hard erection nudged between her thighs.

An erotic energy zapped through her entire system. His mouth claimed hers while his hand began to explore. His fingers made circles at her navel while his lips teased hers. She closed her eyes, savoring everything.

Then his tongue arrived at the peaks of her jutting breasts. His tongue flicked out to lick over one nipple, while his thumb rubbed the other aching bud.

Her eyes flew open and she lifted her head up off the mattress. She had to see what he was doing to make her feel so good. Her gaze latched on to his lips as she watched him drawing her nipple in and out of his mouth.

His tongue laved her sensitive skin as he suckled her. She writhed against him, trying to push her body into his, needing more. Silken ribbons of fevered sensation unfurled straight to her throbbing sex. Her inner muscles contracted.

"I want to feel you inside me, Gibb. I want you now."

He reached for the box of condoms resting on the

bed, ripped it open, yanked one out, but sent the rest of the packets flying around the room.

"Here, let me." She took the condom from him with trembling hands and sheathed his hard shaft.

She positioned him, inviting him in.

He moaned low in his throat, a uniquely masculine sound of pleasure and lowered his body down over hers. He was kissing her again, her mouth, her nose, her eyelids, her ears. He was over her and around her and at last, he was inside of her.

"Sophia," he whispered her name, soft as the ocean waves outside the open window. The one word caressed her ears as he rotated his hips to tease and torment her.

His eyes glowed in a soft light from the tiki torches on the patio shining through the window, his thrusts gentle and slow. He captured her lips, roughly, but lovingly and their mouths clung as he increased the tempo of their mating.

"More," she begged. "Please more."

He quickened the pace. Sophia raised her hips, egging him on.

Soon, she could not tell where he began and she ended. No separation. Their connection was absolute and it filled them in every sense.

She all but hummed with joy. Their oneness made her feel strong and resilient. It rippled through her, stoked her desire.

His body stiffened and she wrapped her legs around his waist, pulling him in as deep as he could go. Release claimed them both and he called out her name in a low, guttural cry.

Sophia awoke sometime later to find herself cradled in the crook of Gibb's arm, his hand gently stroking her hair. Her head was nestled against his chest and she could hear the steady thumping of his heart.

Home. It felt like home in his arms.

No. She must not think like that. Could not think like that. It was simply too dangerous.

The urgency of their previous mating had died down and in its place was a gentle softness. His fingers massaged her scalp, sending sweet shivers skipping down her spine.

She traced the ridges of the scar on his chest with a finger. His lips touched her temple and drew a path of kisses down to her cheek.

Immediately her body responded.

"Enjoy," he murmured, smoothing his palm over her shoulder.

But how could she enjoy when he was running his other hand over her breasts, lightly teasing her nipples? He shifted and his mouth replaced his hand, his tongue sucking gently on her beaded peaks. And there went those exploring fingers, tracing down her midriff and sliding between her thighs.

He didn't make a misstep. Every stroke took the intensity up a notch. He kissed the underside of her chin, his lips wickedly hot. Then he turned her on her side and placed his hip against her butt. He bent her right leg and edged in closer, positioning himself to sink into her from behind.

Now, with him deep inside her, she felt every twitch of his muscles. He lit her up, a match to gasoline.

"Ah, my Sophia," he whispered. "My beautiful, beautiful Sophia."

In that moment, an emotion unlike anything she'd

ever before experienced overtook her. She couldn't
name it, but she felt it to the center of her soul.

He moved purposefully, the rhythm easy and languid. He was, after all, a purposeful man. She whimpered and pressed against him, urging him to pick up
the pace, but he only laughed and went even slower.

The pressure built, tight and heavy. She was acutely
aware of every breath, every pulse beat. He cupped
her buttock as he slid in and out, building momentum,
working toward something grand.

Soft mewling sounds escaped her throat, slipped into
the darkened room to mingle with his pleasure-induced
groans. His mouth burned the back of her neck, hot and
erotic, tender and loving, but he never lost the rhythm.
Their bodies were joined, fused, perfectly matched.
Each movement elicited more delight, more surprise.

Then he rolled onto his back, took her with him,
turning her around until she straddled him. Their gazes
met and Sophia dropped into the exciting comfort of his
eyes. He locked his hands around her waist, helping her
move up and down on his hard, long shaft.

Swept away, she quickened the pace. Gibb met her
challenge, raising his hips up, digging his heels into the
mattress, giving her a ride to end all rides. He kept at it,
chasing her pleasure with a devotion that dizzied her.

Higher and higher he drove her toward climax. She
smiled at him and he laughed with delight. At the peak,
she cried out his name.

He followed right behind her, and together they flew
high into the blue sky, soared the wind currents and
touched the stars.

He held on to her protectively as she buried her face
at his neck. She drew in the scent of him. This was the

smell of their lovemaking. They clung to each other, quivering and spent.

Gibb stroked her, murmured sweet nothings until her heart rate returned to normal and her body had stilled.

"I've never felt so special," she whispered.

"That's because you are special." He lifted her chin, looked deeply into her eyes again. "You are one in a billion, Sophia Cruz."

14

SOPHIA'S PLAN WAS to creep out of the motel room before dawn, sneak like an orchid thief into the night before Gibb awoke. The thought of goodbye choked her up inside, but she'd no more than laid her hand on the doorknob, her clothes clutched to her chest so she could dress in the outer room, when he said, "Running out on me, Amelia?"

She paused, turned back to look at him. He was propped up on his elbows, his hair sexily mussed, his eyes dark and inviting. It took everything she had in her not to crawl back into bed with him and make love to him all over again.

"Um," she said. "I thought I'd just get out of your hair."

He sat up, patted the end of the mattress. "Come here."

She shouldn't go, but damn her she did, creeping back to him, using her red sundress to conceal her nakedness. "What is it?"

"I just wanted you to know that the last two days have been the best of my life."

She laughed. "That's kind of sad. We crash landed on a deserted island, had passion fruit chucked at us by spider monkeys, thwarted orchid thieves—"

"My point exactly. Being with you is fun, Sophia."

"If we were together all the time it wouldn't be like this. It's only because things were strange and new. A big adventure."

He picked up her hand, pressed his lips against her knuckles. "You think the way we steam up the sheets isn't special?"

"It's special." She nodded. "But we come from different worlds."

"Cultural differences can be negotiated with understanding and patience."

"That's not the difference I'm talking about. I'm American enough to bridge that gap."

He stroked her cheek with a finger. "What is it, then?"

"You're rich, I'm not. You're a mover and shaker who is always reaching for the stars. I'm perfectly content spending my life just flying tourists from Libera to Bosque de Los Dioses." She gave him a sad smile. "Although eventually, when you get your transportation system up and running, I won't even have that."

"I told you that you could come work for me."

She stood up, put on the sundress, backed away from him. If he kept touching her, she would agree to anything he asked. "I'm not Cinderella waiting for some handsome prince to sweep me off my feet. I'm not Blondie. I need an equal partnership, not a sugar daddy."

"I wouldn't try to control you."

She had to laugh at that. "Of course you would. You can't help yourself. You control people through your money. That's why money is so important to you. Your best friend can't even live the life he wants without your interference. You simply can't accept that Scott would rather be with the woman he loves than make millions on a project with you. You've got to understand something, Gibb. Money isn't everything."

"But Scott can't love her," he insisted.

"Why not?"

"Because Scott has only known her a month."

"That's a whole lot longer than we've known each other," she said quietly and walked out the door.

ALL THE WAY to Florida, Gibb thought of Sophia.

Everything she'd said about him was true. He did use money to control people. The need to control every outcome was what drove him to make more and more money when he already had more than he could ever spend.

She was also right that they barely knew each other, but he had such strong feelings for her. Feelings he'd never had before about anyone. Was this the way Scott felt about his Jackie? That was a startling thought.

He might not be able to woo Sophia, but after a woman like that, one thing was for sure, he could not go back to Stacy. He tried to call Stacy from the jet to tell her they needed to talk, but he got voice mail and decided to hang up. He'd deal with that later.

His pilot touched down in Miami first where Gibb changed out of the blue T-shirt and khaki shorts he'd bought on Island de Providencia and put on a suit. After that, he returned to the airport and took his jet to Key West, arriving just after two o'clock. He hired a car to take him to Wharf 16 where the wedding was being held on the *Sea Anemone*.

Workers, deep in preparation, scurried to and fro.

Gibb stopped a woman with a clipboard who looked official. "Can you tell me where I might find the groom?"

She pointed behind him.

Gibb turned to see his buddy standing there in his Coast Guard dress blues. He offered up a big smile, but Scott wasn't buying it.

"If you're here to start trouble, just turn around and walk away," Scott growled. "Jackie is the woman I love with all my heart and soul. You're my best friend in the whole world, Gibb, but I will not tolerate one unkind word said against her."

Gibb surrendered.

"If you can't be happy for us, you can go." Scott pointed toward the car Gibb had driven up in.

"I didn't come here to break the two of you up."

Scott stared at him in disbelief. "No?"

"All right, I admit it. I originally came here to try to talk you out of marrying a woman you barely know, but somewhere over the Caribbean Sea—" on a little deserted island to be precise "—I altered my thinking."

Scott crossed his arms over his chest, a suspicious expression on his face. "What happened to cause this change of heart?"

"I understand now."

"Understand?" Scott's brows dipped in a perplexed frown. "Wait. What are you saying? Did you meet someone?"

Gibb thought of Sophia and he clinched his jaw, shrugged.

"There's a woman?" Scott sounded positively gleeful.

"Yes," Gibb forced the word past his lips.

Scott rubbed his palms together. "So what's she like? Tell me everything."

"I don't want to talk about it."

"Ah, I get it. You haven't told her that you love her yet."

"I…" Was he ready to say the *L* word out loud? "It's complicated."

"It's only complicated if you make it complicated."

"I don't really know her," he admitted. And yet, he felt as if he knew her better than he knew anyone else in the world. He knew exactly what happened when he tickled the back of her knee and what she looked like first thing in the morning. He knew she had more courage in her little finger than most people did in their entire bodies. And talk about passion! The woman was off-the-charts passionate—about flying, about orchids, about sex. Whatever she did, she threw herself into it one hundred percent.

"This special woman got a name?" Scott asked.

"Sophia. Sophia Cruz."

"Costa Rican?" Scott guessed.

"Half American by birth, fully Costa Rican by nature."

"Ah," he said. "She's laidback."

"Yeah."

"Easygoing."

"That, too."

"Exactly what a hard-driving guy like you needs."

No denying it. Sophia had taught him so many things in such a short amount of time. Chief among them was that smelling the roses was worth slowing down for and that money truly wasn't everything. Other people had tried to tell him that, but none had shown him the way Sophia had.

With Sophia, he finally saw the path to a different life. One he never knew existed.

"What does Sophia do for a living?"

"She's a pilot."

"Skilled," Scott said. "And I'm guessing smart as a whip."

"She is."

"So what are you going to do about it?"

He shook his head. "Nothing."

Scott's mouth dropped open, then he snapped it shut and scoffed. "Unbelievable."

"What?"

"You have love in the palm of your hand and you're going to walk away from her?"

Was he? Gibb wasn't sure anymore.

Scott looked sad and disappointed. "You're a tougher case than I thought."

Why was it so difficult for him to admit he was falling in love? "Like I said, I don't really know her."

"Yeah?" Scott cocked an eyebrow. "Let me put it to you in a language you understand. What do you do before you fund a product or invest an upstart business?"

"Figure profit and loss."

"So let's make it all about money since that's your emotional currency."

"I resent that." He felt as if he were choking and loosened his tie.

"Have you changed in some fundamental way?"

"I'm working on it. I'm trying."

"Okay, tell me this. What do you like most about Sophia?"

Gibb smiled. "I like how calm she stays in the face of a crisis and how everything makes her smile. When she smiles it's like the sun coming out after a month of rain. And she wears this sassy pink straw cowboy hat cocked back on her head and she's got long, thick, straight jet-black hair. How she doesn't allow me to snow her with nonsense. Scott, she has the most amazing power to see right through me, to the kid I used to be. You know, how I was before my mom married James and I started turning myself inside out to prove I was worthy of James's love and respect. Sophia puts me in touch with that kid who I've tried so hard to run away from. She..." He paused to take a breath.

"Sounds very special," Scott finished quietly.

"Yes. Yes, she is."

"Now let's look at the loss side of the column. What is the downside of pursuing a relationship with Sophia?"

"We're night and day. She's down-to-earth and I drive a Bentley. She lives in a secluded mountain range in Costa Rica and I own homes in Miami, Santa Barbara and Aspen."

"You didn't always."

"I know."

"Here's the big question. What is it that you are so afraid of?"

Gibb snorted. "Honestly?"

"I've found it's the best policy."

"I'm afraid I don't know how to be ordinary anymore. I'm out of touch with the real world, Scott."

"When was the last time you did something ordinary?"

Gibb grinned. "I made campfire s'mores with So-phia."

"She's good for you."

"I know."

"So what are you still doing here, Gibb?"

"I was hoping you'd let me be your best man, unless you've got someone else for the task. Ah, hell, what am I saying? Of course you've already got a best man—"

"I do," Scott said, "and I'm looking right at him."

"You didn't ask someone else already?" Gibb was surprised at the rush of gratitude that filled him. Scott was not only forgiving him for his behavior but he still considered him his best man.

"I did ask my dad's closest friend Carl to step in, but he said if you showed up and wanted the job, he'd happily serve as an usher instead."

"Really?" It was ridiculous how happy this was making him. He clamped his teeth together to keep his eyes from misting up. Scott was a damn good friend. Better than he deserved.

Scott clapped him on the shoulder. "I hoped you would change your mind and come to your senses and wish the best for me and my bride."

"Thanks, guy," Gibb said, and then shut his mouth before he got choked up.

Scott touched the platinum bracelet on his right wrist. "Remember what we said the day we bought these?"

Gibb's fingers went to his own bare wrist. "Blood brothers forever."

"Hey, what happened to your chain?"

"Long story. I'll tell you at the reception."

"Doesn't matter, does it? The chain is just a symbol. It's what it represents that counts. I'm just so glad you're here."

"Me, too."

"C'mon. I'll introduce you to Jackie, but after the wedding, I want you to do something for me."

"Anything. You name it."

"Get yourself on that corporate jet and get your ass back to Costa Rica and tell Sophia that you're in love with her."

"What if…" Gibb swallowed hard and then finally voiced what he had feared most. "What if she doesn't feel the same way about me?"

"You're good at taking risks, but this doesn't sound like a risk at all to me. The list of profits is long and there's honestly nothing on the loss side of the equation."

"But if I tell her I love her and she doesn't reciprocate I don't think I can stand losing her."

"Buddy," Scott said. "What if she does love you right back? Do you really want to walk away and cut your losses before you ever find out?"

SIX HOURS LATER, after Scott and his bride had sailed off on the *Sea Anemone,* Gibb paced the lobby of a private hangar at Key West International Airport. He was waiting for a lightning storm to pass before he and his pilot could take off for Costa Rica.

He'd only been there a few minutes, but he was terrible at waiting.

Calm down, amigo, where's the fire? Sophia's laughing voice whispered to him.

Immediately, he smiled and stopped pacing. Blowing out a deep breath, he plunked down in a lounge chair to watch the evening news on the big-screen TV. At this hour of the night, he was the only one around.

"In financial news," the anchor said, "communications giant Fisby Corp has announced they own the patent to an innovative ecological transportation system destined to change the way the world travels." On the TV screen there was a detailed picture of the travel system that was eerily similar to the one that Gibb had invested in. "Stay tuned for more on the story after the commercial break."

What? Not again!

Gibb jumped to his feet, unable to believe what he'd just heard. Despite all his precautions, a corporate spy had zinged him again! How in the hell had Fisby managed to get a patent through before his inventor?

The broadcast resumed and the news anchor picked up the story again. The camera flashed to a live action shot of the CEO of Fisby Corp climbing into his stretch limo with a beautiful blonde woman on his arm—a woman that Gibb knew intimately. The woman who loved giving his black credit card a good workout.

Stacy.

She was the corporate spy all along. He'd been sleeping with the enemy.

Stunned, he stared at the TV, waited for the anger to hit him, braced for feelings of betrayal and indignation, but oddly, those feelings didn't come.

He sat back down on the chair. Well, what do you know? Stacy was the corporate spy. He had to give credit where credit was due. She'd certainly pulled the wool over his eyes.

All at once, the situation tickled his funny bone.

Gibb threw back his head and laughed, laughed until

fat tears rolled down his face. Laughed until the receptionist behind the desk gave him a strange look. Two years' worth of work and hundreds of millions of dollars down the tubes and he didn't even care.

"Thank you, Stacy," he told the screen. "You just let me out of a prison of my own making."

Free. For the first time since he'd sold his Zimdiggy game app, he felt free.

15

"WHY ARE you so mopey, *mi hija?*" Her father kissed Sophia's head as she sat at the kitchen table staring out the window.

She reached up to touch her father's face, felt uneven patches of beard mixed with smooth skin. Since he'd been losing his sight, he did a patchwork job of shaving himself, but he was fiercely independent and refused to let anyone else shave him. "How do you know I'm mopey, Poppy?"

"I need eyes to know when my youngest *niña* is sad? How blind do you think I am? You do not sing. There is no smile in your voice. You have been like this since you returned from your failed trip to Key West. What is wrong, *mi hija?*"

How could she tell her father that ever since she left Gibb three days ago in the bungalow at Island de Providencia, she felt as if she'd been slogging through a fog thicker than the daily mist surrounding Bosque de Los Dioses?

She had discovered firsthand that the downside of

great passion was a shattered heart if things did not work out. Passion was not all it was cracked up to be.

But as tempting as it might have been to act as if nothing had happened on that island and slip back into her easy relationship with Emilio, she simply could not bring herself to do it. Once she had tasted real passion, she could never settle for little more than pleasant companionship, even if she and Gibb were not destined to be together.

The day she'd gotten home, she went to see Emilio and told him that while she valued their friendship, she could not in good conscience keep dating him. It turned out that he had been feeling the same way.

"You can still patch things up with Emilio," her father murmured. "It is not too late."

"But, Poppy, I do not love him."

"Ah," her father said, "I understand. You love another."

"Yes," she whispered, "I do, but he doesn't love me back."

"Then he is a very stupid man."

"I think he's just afraid to let himself love."

"Then he is very, very stupid. Love is nothing to be afraid of."

She drew her knees to her chest, hugged herself. "It hurts so much, Poppy."

"I know, *mi hija*." He squeezed her hand tightly and shuffled off to the living room, leaving her alone with her thoughts.

Sophia dropped her head into her hands. She had been such a fool, hoping against all hope that somehow she had a chance with Gibb. Loco. She was loco. She knew that, but she could not stop thinking about him.

Misery rolled around inside her like a boulder, crashing and smashing, doing irreparable damage. She closed her eyes and tried to take a deep breath, but the pain was so big she could barely do more than suck in a whistle of air through her teeth.

The previous evening, Josie had come over with a weak smile and a big box of tissues. She'd cried and talked and it had helped a little, but the sadness that seeped into her bones was there to stay. After her sister left, she watched her mother's old VHS tape of *To Have and Have Not,* and bawled her eyes out when the crucial line came. Did you ever really get over a broken heart?

She reached for the tissues Josie had left on the table the night before and considered whether to go for the beer in the fridge or the ice cream in the freezer, when her cell phone rang.

For one idiotic second, she thought, *Gibb!*

She snatched her phone from her pocket, looked at the caller ID and her hopes vanished. It was her aunt Kristi from Ventura.

"Hello?" she mumbled, barely able to hold the sniffles at bay.

"Sophia, honey, Josie told me you've just had your first broken heart."

"Oh, Auntie," she said and the sobs overtook her.

"Sweetheart," Kristi said. "You just need to get away and I want to give you a giant hug. Come on up and stay with us for as long as you need to. Your cousins and I will meet you at the airport."

She'd seen her mother's family every couple of years and the invitation couldn't have come at a better time. Gibb would be returning to the mountain soon to work on his secret project. It would be so hard to be near him and not give in to the attraction. Much better to leave the country and give herself some distance to get over him. Besides, once his project was complete, she would be out of a job. Maybe now was the time to look into other opportunities for employment. Who knew what the future might hold?

After all, she was lucky. She had something Gibb did not have, a large supportive family who loved her enough to rally around her when she was suffering. She was richer than he would ever be.

"Are you coming?" her aunt asked.

"Yes, Auntie," she said firmly before she had a chance to talk herself out of it. "Yes, thank you for inviting me. I'm on my way."

THE MINUTE GIBB'S plane touched down in Libera in the wee hours on Wednesday morning, four days after he'd last seen Sophia, he realized he had no idea where she lived. He had her cell phone number, but he didn't want to do this over the phone. He had to see her face-to-face.

After the Fisby Corp announcement, he'd had some things to take care of, but once business was out of the way, he'd come back to Cordillera of Tilarán as quickly as he could.

He stalked up to the operations center that he knew she flew out of, but the doors were locked and he did not see El Diablo on the tarmac behind the ten-foot chain fence. For a second, he panicked, worrying that she had not made it home from Island de Providencia and he cursed himself for not calling sooner to make sure she was safe. But he'd wanted to surprise her.

Calm down. Her plane is probably in a hanger.

Now what? He couldn't wait until the operations center opened. He had to see her right now. What to do? He paced back and forth.

Maybe he should just call her? But what if she refused his call? Or worse, answered the phone only to tell him that she did not want to see him.

An old white Ford pickup truck drove up to the center and a man got out.

"Hola!" Gibb greeted him forcefully. "I am looking for Señorita Sophia Cruz. Do you know where I can find her?"

The man shrugged. "Not here."

Well, clearly not, since the place was closed up. Frustrated, Gibb ran a hand through his hair. "Do you know where I can find her?"

"Are you a customer? If you want to hire a plane to Bosque de Los Dioses, give me thirty minutes and I can take you."

He grasped the man's arm, stared at him hard. "No, I want Sophia. Sophia is the one I need. The only one."

The man raised an eyebrow. "I'm sorry, *señor*. She has moved to California."

SOPHIA WAS WALKING along Ventura beach at sunset. Overhead, seagulls cried. It was better here than at home. Here, she did not keep imagining she saw Gibb every time she turned a corner.

Except there was a tall muscular blond man approaching her. Her pulse leaped.

Don't be silly. It's not him. He's in Bosque de Los Dioses working on his precious project.

Still, her ridiculous imagination couldn't help pointing out that he had a beach home in Santa Barbara and Ventura wasn't all that far south of it.

A kid was running along the sand with a bright purple bat-wing kite. The wind caught it, lifted it high. Sophia stopped to watch the boy, appreciating the child's love of a simple activity like kite flying.

"I haven't flown a kite since I was that age," said a voice behind her, a very familiar voice.

Sophia turned to see that the blond man she'd caught a glimpse of earlier was indeed Gibb.

"Hello, Sophia," he said softly.

"What…what are you doing here?"

"Looking for you."

She swallowed hard. "Me?"

He stepped closer. Tension hung heavily in the air. "You."

"Why are you looking for me?"

"I found out you left Bosque de Los Dioses. I chased you away from your home."

"If the invention you are investing in takes off, I won't have a job there anyway. It's better that I start a new life now. Begin adjusting."

"So you're not running away to avoid seeing me?"

Unable to hold his gaze, she turned to look out at the ocean. "I…it's less painful not being near you."

"I came to tell you something." Gibb reached for her. Lightly, gently, he cupped her elbow in one hand, cradled her chin in the other and guided her face back to his.

Hope. So much darn hope crowded her chest. "And what is that?"

"That you were right."

"What about?" A million emotions jolted through Sophia like tiny shocks of electricity.

"Everything." He stared at her, into her. "About me

having to be in control. About there being more to life than money."

"What caused you to realize that?"

"Well, for one thing, the corporate spies caught me again. They got a patent for the green transportation technology I'd invested in before we did."

"I'm sorry to hear that. How do these spies keep stealing your secrets when you are so careful?"

Gibb snorted. "Because I was sleeping with the enemy."

Sophia cocked her head. "I do not understand."

"Stacy. She was the corporate spy. How do you like them apples?"

"She betrayed you!"

"And ran up quite a bill on my credit card while doing it."

"Good thing she is not here right now." Sophia scowled. "Or I would have to call her out for hurting you."

Gibb smiled. "I have no doubt that you would. You could take her, too." He winked. "I've seen you in action. You are a woman to be reckoned with."

She notched her chin up. "When something or someone I love is threatened, you bet I am."

Suddenly, it occurred to her that she'd inadvertently told him she loved him. She slapped her fingers over her mouth, tried to figure out how to backtrack without making things worse.

His smile widened.

"And the other thing?"

He drew her to him. "What other thing?"

"That made you realize I was right?"

"Losing you, Sophia. I love you. And it broke my heart when you walked out on me."

"It broke mine, too," she murmured.

His gray eyes searched her face. "I missed you fiercely."

"I missed you, too."

He kissed her then, running one hand up the nape of her neck, spearing his fingers through her hair. A gust of wind blew against them. The sun was sinking fast. The kid with the kite was hauling it in for the night.

"Did you get to Key West in time to stop your friend from getting married?" she asked.

"I did."

"You must be very happy. You got what you wanted."

He moved closer to her. "I didn't try to break Scott and Jackie up."

"No?"

"No," he lowered his voice.

"Why not?"

"For one thing, I saw how happy she made him and for another..."

"What?" Sophia prodded.

"I realized how completely happy you make me."

"But we hardly know each other."

"Oh," Gibb said. "That's where you're wrong. I know you have the cutest little birthmark on your left hip and that you can fix a broken rudder cable with a platinum bracelet. I know that I always want you on my side whether it's a passion-fruit fight with spider monkeys or stopping orchid thieves with snare nooses."

"That was fun, wasn't it?"

"I know that I can't get enough of you." He dipped

his head to kiss her again. "And that I want to wake up every morning of my life to find you lying next to me."

"That sounds very nice." She plucked at the collar of his shirt.

"There's a reason I didn't come looking for you sooner," he said.

"And what reason is that?"

"I had business to take care of since the project at Bosque de Los Dioses is a no go."

"What are you going to do now?" She planted a kiss on his neck at the V of his collar.

"I thought I'd take your advice, stop worrying about making money and instead worry about having fun and doing what pleases me."

"Mmm," she said. "That sounds very fun."

"And I want to start by making love to you."

"I definitely like the sound of that."

He bent and swept her off her feet, scooping her into his arms and carrying her down the beach. She wrapped her arms around his neck, never once took her gaze off him. Her heart was overflowing with joy and a hundred other wonderful feelings.

"I have an idea," he said.

"About what?"

"A new game app."

Sophia smiled. "You're going back to creating games?"

"My first love," he said, staring deeply into her eyes.

"What will you call this one?" she murmured, snuggling her face against his chest.

"Sophia and the Orchid Thieves."

She laughed. Would this man always surprise her so? "Terrific. Tell me about the game."

"Well," he said, "there's this amazing girl named Sophia and she flies her own airplane and she goes on exciting adventures."

"Sounds like a superhero."

"Oh, Sophia is much tougher than a superhero."

"So does Sophia go on these adventures all on her own?"

"No. She's got a handsome sidekick."

"What's his name?"

"I don't know yet. You can name him if you want."

"Gibb will do," she said. "And he's a savvy, charming billionaire, with a hint of international intrigue."

"Are you sure? Is that the man you really want for Sophia?"

"Darling," she told him. "I love you. There is no other."

Epilogue

*Former venture capitalist Gibb Martin has re-
turned to his roots and, by doing so, he has sur-
passed his previous standing at 1153 on our list
three years ago by a full one thousand positions
with the release of his sensational new gaming
app. Sophia and the Orchid Thieves.*

*Martin says, "The credit for my success goes
entirely to my beautiful wife, Sophia. I'm a better
man because of her."*

*We think Martin is being too humble, reviews
for Sophia and the Orchid Thieves have garnered
a unanimous thumbs-up from the gaming com-
munity. But no one can deny that his feisty Costa
Rican bride has caused a marked change in Martin who shifted his focus from business to pleasure after Fisby Corp scooped him three times in
two years. Most recently by getting to market first
with a transportation system that was supposed
to revolutionize the way people travel.*

*Unfortunately for Fisby, the invention had a
huge design flaw and the entire project had to*

*be scrapped. Maybe that will serve as a lesson
to Fisby that it's better to come up with your own
ideas than to appropriate them from others. Many
were surprised when Martin did not pursue legal
action against Fisby but not Martin's adopted father, real estate mogul, James Martin.*

*"Gibb is a changed man," says the senior Mar-
tin. "Finding love has altered the way he looks
at the world. I couldn't be prouder of my son."*

*If skyrocketing sales of Sophia and the Or-
chid Thieves is any indication, love is surely the
way to go.*

—Wealth Maker Magazine

"THEY CAN SAY THAT a hundred times and not be wrong,"
Gibb said, taking the magazine away from Sophia and
settling down on the sofa beside her in their treetop
bungalow amidst the clouds of Cordillera of Tilarán.

"What part?" she teased, cradling her swollen belly.
"That the sales of Sophia and the Orchid Thieves are
skyrocketing?"

"The part about love surely being the way to go."

"Uh-huh."

"Who knew three short years ago that one airplane
ride to stop a wedding would start all this?" Gibb rested
his head on her belly.

She smiled and placed her hand over his.

"Imagine." He raised his head and looked deeply
into her eyes. "A son."

"Imagine," she murmured. "A husband who gets to
stay home all day doing what he loves."

"Imagine." He laughed. "Having a mother who flies

through the air doing what she loves and can single-handedly fight off orchid thieves."

"We are the two luckiest people in the world." Sophia's heart was full to bursting.

"I do love creating games," Gibb said. "But I love you more and that love grows bigger each day and will soon include our children, too."

"Only one so far."

"Ah," he said, "but we are just getting started."

"And to think we owe it all to a crash landing." She laughed.

Gibb pulled her into his arms and gave her a long, deep kiss and Sophia realized that she truly had the best of both worlds. Red-hot passion and a true partnership destined to last a lifetime.

* * * * *

Waking Up To You

Gently pushing her, Oliver ordered, "Go."

All because he needed *her* to be the one who walked away
and ended this before it really began? As if he had no free will?
As if unless she did, he wouldn't be able to stop himself from
doing to her exactly what she'd practically dared him to do?

*You don't want him to do it, either, remember? You know you
can't do this.*

No. She might want Oliver, and having sex with him might
even be worth what she would go through afterward if people
found out. But she needed to cool this, here and now. She had
to be the one who walked away.

Which still wasn't going to be easy.

"I'm telling you, you really don't want to watch me walking
up those stairs."

"Yes. I really do."

"You'll regret it."

"Hell, I already regret it," he said, tunneling both his hands
through his hair this time, leaving it more tousled than before.

"Not as much as you're about to."

Without another word, she spun around again, squared her shoulders, stiffened her spine and ascended the stairs. He stood below, watching her, and when she reached the fourth one, she couldn't help pausing to glance over her shoulder at him.

"Oh, Oliver, do you want to know why I didn't want to walk up the stairs until you left?"

He didn't reply, just gave her an inscrutable look.

She told him anyway. "Because of this."

Candace took another step, knowing she'd reached the point of no return. Knowing full well he could now see what she was *not* wearing beneath her robe.

She wished she could say his strangled, guttural cry of helpless frustration made her feel better about walking away from what she sensed could be the best sex of her life.

But she just couldn't.

Pick up WAKING UP TO YOU by Leslie Kelly, available April 23 wherever you buy Harlequin Blaze books.

As a special treat to you, you will also find Leslie's classic story *Overexposed* in the same volume. That's 2 great books for 1 great price!

REQUEST YOUR FREE BOOKS!
2 FREE NOVELS PLUS 2 FREE GIFTS!

red-hot reads!

YES! Please send me 2 FREE Harlequin® Blaze™ novels and my 2 FREE gifts (gifts are worth about $10). After receiving them, if I don't wish to receive any more books, I can return the shipping statement marked "cancel." If I don't cancel, I will receive 4 brand-new novels every month and be billed just $4.49 per book in the U.S. or $4.96 per book in Canada. That's a savings of at least 14% off the cover price. It's quite a bargain. Shipping and handling is just 50¢ per book in the U.S. and 75¢ per book in Canada.* I understand that accepting the 2 free books and gifts places me under no obligation to buy anything. I can always return a shipment and cancel at any time. Even if I never buy another book, the two free books and gifts are mine to keep forever.

150/350 HDN FV42

Name (PLEASE PRINT)

Address Apt. #

City State/Prov. Zip/Postal Code

Signature (if under 18, a parent or guardian must sign)

Mail to the **Harlequin® Reader Service:**
IN U.S.A.: P.O. Box 1867, Buffalo, NY 14240-1867
IN CANADA: P.O. Box 609, Fort Erie, Ontario L2A 5X3

Want to try two free books from another line?
Call 1-800-873-8635 or visit www.ReaderService.com.

* Terms and prices subject to change without notice. Prices do not include applicable taxes. Sales tax applicable in N.Y. Canadian residents will be charged applicable taxes. Offer not valid in Quebec. This offer is limited to one order per household. Not valid for current subscribers to Harlequin Blaze books. All orders subject to credit approval. Credit or debit balances in a customer's account(s) may be offset by any other outstanding balance owed by or to the customer. Please allow 4 to 6 weeks for delivery. Offer available while quantities last.

Your Privacy—The Harlequin® Reader Service is committed to protecting your privacy. Our Privacy Policy is available online at www.ReaderService.com or upon request from the Harlequin Reader Service.

We make a portion of our mailing list available to reputable third parties that offer products we believe may interest you. If you prefer that we not exchange your name with third parties, or if you wish to clarify or modify your communication preferences, please visit us at www.ReaderService.com/consumerchoice or write to us at Harlequin Reader Service Preference Service, P.O. Box 9062, Buffalo, NY 14269. Include your complete name and address.

HB13R

Double your reading pleasure with Harlequin Blaze!

As a special treat to you, all Harlequin Blaze books in May will include a new story, plus a classic story by the same author, including...

Jennifer LaBrecque

Locate the explosive. Defuse or safely detonate it. It's a job that takes cojones, and one wrong move could land marine demolitions expert Lars Reinhardt in the hurt locker...or in the morgue. But it takes a leave in Good Riddance, Alaska, for Lars to meet his greatest—and prickliest—challenge yet, Delphie Reynolds. And he'll need more than charm to disarm this stunning nurse....

Pick up *Northern Rebel* by *Jennifer LaBrecque* and also enjoy her classic story ***Daring in the Dark*** in the same volume!

AVAILABLE APRIL 23
wherever you buy Harlequin Blaze books.